Lord, please don't let anyone have been inside.

Gary headed toward the EMT wagon. Rounding the corner, he met a paramedic moving toward the burning house. Gary touched the man's arm. "Was anyone in the house?"

"Only her." The EMT nodded at a woman with hair as red as the flames devouring the house.

Gary hated this part of the job—having to ask questions and probe when people were hurting or grieving. He went over. "Ma'am? I'm Gary Anderson, acting sheriff. I need your statement. Can you tell me what happened?"

Lifting her head she set her chin. "Yes. Someone set this."

"You think this was deliberate?" She was confused, obviously. "Ms. Harris, I'm sure you're very upset, but—"

"Yes, I'm upset, but I'm n̶o̶t̶ ... ...one deliberately."

"Why would you t̶h̶i̶n̶k̶

"Because just this ... ... call telling me to leave."

Books by Robin Caroll

Love Inspired Suspense

Bayou Justice
Bayou Corruption
Bayou Judgment
Bayou Paradox
Bayou Betrayal

ROBIN CAROLL

Born and raised in Louisiana, Robin Caroll is Southern to a fault. Her passion has always been to tell stories to entertain others. When she isn't writing, Robin spends time with her husband of nineteen years, her three beautiful daughters and their four character-filled pets at home—in the South, where else? An avid reader herself, Robin loves hearing from and chatting with other readers. Although her favorite genre to read is mystery/suspense, of course, she'll read just about any good story. Except historicals! To learn more about this author of Deep South mysteries of suspense to inspire your heart, visit Robin's Web site at www.robincaroll.com.

BAYOU BETRAYAL

ROBIN CAROLL

Steeple Hill®

Published by Steeple Hill Books™

If you purchased this book without a cover you should be aware that this book is stolen property. It was reported as "unsold and destroyed" to the publisher, and neither the author nor the publisher has received any payment for this "stripped book."

STEEPLE HILL BOOKS

Steeple Hill®

Recycling programs
for this product may
not exist in your area.

ISBN-13: 978-0-373-44323-9
ISBN-10:   0-373-44323-4

BAYOU BETRAYAL

Copyright © 2009 by Robin Miller

All rights reserved. Except for use in any review, the reproduction or utilization of this work in whole or in part in any form by any electronic, mechanical or other means, now known or hereafter invented, including xerography, photocopying and recording, or in any information storage or retrieval system, is forbidden without the written permission of the editorial office, Steeple Hill Books, 233 Broadway, New York, NY 10279 U.S.A.

This is a work of fiction. Names, characters, places and incidents are either the product of the author's imagination or are used fictitiously, and any resemblance to actual persons, living or dead, business establishments, events or locales is entirely coincidental.

This edition published by arrangement with Steeple Hill Books.

® and TM are trademarks of Steeple Hill Books, used under license. Trademarks indicated with ® are registered in the United States Patent and Trademark Office, the Canadian Trade Marks Office and in other countries.

www.SteepleHill.com

Printed in U.S.A.

You are my hiding place; you will protect
me from trouble and surround me
with songs of deliverance.
—*Psalms* 32:7

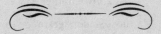

For my dearest siblings: Tom, BB, Bek and Bubba, and the two I'm blessed to have gained by marriage—Robert and Lisa—I thank each of you for your love, support and encouragement. You are a daily blessing in my life.

Acknowledgments:

My most sincere gratitude to:

Krista Stroever, who is so much more than just my editor—I'm honored to call her friend. And her assistant, Elizabeth Mazer, who puts in so much time, energy and talent into my books.

Kelly Mortimer, for being my "soul" agent.

Colleen Coble, for continued friendship, love and belief in me.

The boards of ACFW for such support and outpouring of love.

Camy, Cara, Cheryl, Dineen, Heather, Lisa, Pammer, Ronie and Trace, for input and support. Love y'all.

Billy Wyatt, for answering my endless questions about biodiesel with such grace!

My family for continued encouragement: Mom & Papa, Krystina, Brandon & Rachel, Bill & Connie, and all the rest of the clan!

My daughters—Emily, Remington and Isabella—I love you all so much.

All my love to my husband, Case, for his continued support and prayers in following my dreams and heart.

All glory to my Lord and Savior, Jesus Christ.

PROLOGUE

Just holding the match against the strike-plate caused him to tremble. Knowing what would come, having that ultimate control.

His heart pounded, adrenaline pumping through his veins.

There was something lyrical about striking a match. The scratching, followed by the sizzle. White smoke spiraling upward. The comforting aroma of sulfur tickling his nostrils. He took a deep breath, inhaling the smell that energized him.

All too soon, the match burned to his fingertips. With a slow puff of air, he extinguished the flame. He always brought a whole box of matches, going through several before he finally let the beast loose. Once the fire was released from his hand, it roared and devoured like a lion on a rampage. Too fast.

And he could never stay long enough to watch the monster destroy. Not without risk.

He was good at his chosen profession, passionate and thorough. Not once had he gotten caught. Well, there was one short stint in prison, but it had nothing to do with arson and only served to give him more connections, more business. Stupid cops—they'd never fingered him for a single blaze.

Lighting another match extinguished the annoyance he felt when it came to the police. For many years he'd perfected his craft. Honed his skill. Expanded his talents. All because of his love for the deadly flames.

He dropped the match and stared at the house in front of him, the one he'd already coated in accelerant. There'd be no mistakes here, either. He was clever, using a local accelerant, one that would make the police focus on a local angle. His boss would be pleased.

He was that good.

Crouching, he held the final match against the strike-plate. This was it.

If only his employer had known he'd have done the job for free. Just for the thrill of releasing the fiery monster. But he sure wouldn't turn down the money. After all, he wasn't brainless.

He struck the match, inhaled for a moment, letting the flame move down the stick. When it almost kissed his fingers, he dropped it onto the fuel trail he'd poured so carefully.

Flames shot along the bayou and the fire snaked in a ring around the house.

Crackling, popping, sizzling.

He straightened and shoved his hands in his jacket pockets. With a final glance at the flames licking the wood, he headed to his car.

Another successful beast unleashed.

ONE

Her throat burned, the acidic sensation ripping Monique Harris from a sound sleep. Disoriented, she swallowed against a stinging throat. The pungent smell of smoke accosted her. She held her throbbing head and sat up, fighting to clear the sleep from her mind. She glanced around the room, heart thudding. This wasn't her bedroom.

Reality washed over her. This *was* hers. Her new house in Lagniappe, Louisiana, where she'd celebrated the New Year by settling in. The place she'd run to when she needed to start over. She sucked in air.

Breathing was nearly impossible. The air hung thick…heavy… hot.

Recognition and realization slammed her gut. Fire!

Bolting out of bed, she ran, tripping over the tangle of bed-covers as she pushed from her bedroom into the hallway. Dense smoke swirled in the air, forming a wall. Monique covered her nose and mouth with her hand and stumbled along the hall. Her knee connected with boxes piled in the walkway, knocking her down. Pulling herself up, she fought to focus. She had to get her bearings, had to keep her wits about her.

Deep orange flames sizzled everywhere—heat overwhelmed her. How long had the fire been burning while she slept?

An underlying stench invaded her nostrils. A surge of raw fear pulsated inside her, tingling down into her limbs. She moved to lean against the wall, but heat seared her back. She jumped away, staggering.

Off in the distance, sirens wailed their approach. Someone must've called 9-1-1. Help would reach her soon, but she had to get out of the house. *Now.* No time to wait.

Monique stumbled toward the front door. Flames shot out from the living room and stopped her in her tracks. Her bare heels burned against the hardwood floor. She backed away and stumbled blindly toward the kitchen.

The only other door out of the house.

Heat scorched the soles of her feet as she ran through the thick smoke. She coughed and gagged, eyes burning and tears spilling down her cheeks. She wasn't going to make it. Not on her own. It'd been a long time since she asked for help, especially from God. A long time since she'd gotten angry with Him. She still wasn't ready to let go of her anger, but she cried out now.

God, please don't let me die. Not like this.

Sheetrock fell from the ceiling. She screamed and crouched, covering her head with her arms. Wallpaper peeled into crumbling piles of embers. Fear spurred her onward.

She dropped to all fours, the hot floor digging into her knees and hands, burning. Her vision blurred against the smoke. Get to the back door. Get out of the house.

The muscles in her arms and legs cramped as she struggled toward the kitchen. Sheer determination propelled her forward.

Please, God. Help me.

Coughing, she finally reached the kitchen. She stood to reach the doorknob and spied her purse lying on the kitchen counter. Kent's Bible was inside it. In one fluid motion, she snared the bag and tossed the strap over her shoulder. Covering the doorknob with her flannel pajama top, she flung open the kitchen door.

January night air cooled her lungs and throat. Monique paused to gulp in the freshness. Then sweat beads settled on her upper lip and brow as heat streaked across her face, like sitting too close to an open campfire. The only problem was the campfire was her house. Smoke billowed from the open door, suffusing the bayou in a gray haze. She pushed herself to keep moving.

Sirens screeched louder, closer. Her nerves knotted, and she wanted to throw up but knew she had to keep moving. Had to get away from the burning house.

She tripped down the four wooden steps and landed on the ground with a resounding thud. Coughing and sputtering, Monique felt like her lungs were going to come up. Nausea swept over her in waves. Still she pressed on, crawling toward her vehicle, ignoring the gravel digging into her bare, stinging palms.

A fire truck, lights strobing and siren wailing, whipped into the driveway and screeched to a halt. Gravel dust mixed with the smoke pouring from the open kitchen door, filling the air with a dense cloud. An EMT unit followed. In record time, the paramedics had her in the back of their wagon with an oxygen mask over her face. The medic held it tight, and she inhaled several times before removing the mask.

A fireman touched her shoulder. "Is there anyone else in the house?"

His words sounded muffled against the hum of the fire and the bustle of activity around her. "What?"

"In the house. Is there anyone still inside?"

"No. I live alone." Ever since Kent had been murdered, she had no one. Loneliness hit her anew. Would the mourning ever end?

The blood pressure cuff squeezed her arm as the paramedic measured her blood pressure. Monique blinked several times, washing out the burning feeling along with solution they'd placed into her eyes. The cuff came off with a rip of Velcro.

She stared at her home going up in flames. What a way to start the New Year. What caused it? Faulty wiring? No, the inspector had checked that. She hadn't even turned on the oven or stove. Smoke swirled as flaming beams crashed.

The fire burned hot. And fast. Wait a minute…

She bolted from the back of the EMT wagon, horror settling over her. "No!"

A firefighter grabbed her arm and jerked her away from the popping flames. "Ma'am, you can't go in there."

She froze, hot tears burning her scorched face.

The pieces quickly fell into place. The out-of-control fire. The smell. And the phone call she'd received just the other day. It hadn't been a prank after all. She'd been warned. This wasn't an accident. This had been planned, set. This was arson.

Someone didn't want her in Lagniappe.

"Deputy, we got a 9-1-1 call reporting a burning house." Missy, the dispatcher, stood in the sheriff's doorway, her platinum-blond hair looking as frazzled as she sounded.

Deputy Gary Anderson, the acting sheriff, let out a long sigh. Only January 2, and already a call? So much for a quiet two weeks catching up on paperwork and getting the office organized. "Is it bad?"

"According to the neighbor, the place was engulfed in flames before they even noticed."

Gary shoved to his feet, reaching for his radio. "Is it too much to hope the place was vacant?"

"Sorry, Deputy. It's the house out on Bridges Lane that young woman moved into just last week."

"Well, I'll be." He snatched his keys off the desk. "The old Pittman place?"

"That's the one."

"I'm on my way." He made quick strides out the front door and across the lot to the cruiser parked in the sheriff's space.

Anticipation soared in his chest, despite the potential tragedy looming over the bayou. Sheriff Bubba Theriot was on vacation and as acting sheriff, Gary had all the responsibilities that went along with the title. He'd better write a report, get it filed, then have cleanup ordered before the sheriff returned. This could be his chance to make an impression. A good one.

Two weeks—that's all Gary had to prove himself. The sheriff had taken his wife, Tara, to New Orleans to visit her sister and the new baby. Bubba was a good man, Gary would never say otherwise, but he didn't seem to put much stock in Gary's abilities to handle matters on his own. This was Gary's opportunity, maybe his only one. And he'd prove himself worthy.

With siren screaming and lights blazing, he raced down the roads through his beloved town. He'd grown up just outside the city limits of Lagniappe, the only child of a widowed mother. She'd worked a multitude of small jobs—cleaning other people's houses, doing ironing from their little two-bedroom rental, waitressing at the small diner—all to support herself and her son. College had never been an option for Gary, but his determination to make something of himself wouldn't allow that to stop him. He'd applied himself, completed correspondence courses on criminal justice and had been hired on as a deputy. But he still hadn't earned the respect he needed.

Not yet. But maybe now…

With the increased population of Lagniappe over the past year, the parish had decided the sheriff's office could justify appointing a chief deputy and hiring a regular deputy for replacement. Gary had the experience and seniority for the position over Deputy Tim Marsh. Sheriff Theriot had already hired another deputy—Mike Fontenot, previous bartender at the jazz club and a former MP with the Marines—but he hadn't made the decision about who would be chief deputy. Now Gary pressed the accelerator harder in his anticipation.

He arrived on the scene amid chaos. Red and white flashed over the bayou from the lights atop the fire trucks. Water shot from hoses at odd angles and filled the air with steam. Firefighters rushed about, barking orders and moving equipment. But the focal point of activity was the home engulfed in flames. Gary's eyes burned from the smoke.

Lord, please don't let anyone have been inside.

He parked and headed toward the EMT wagon, weaving out of the way of the firefighters. Rounding the corner of the vehicle, he met a paramedic moving toward the burning house. Gary touched the man's arm and kept his voice strong and full of authority. "Was anyone in the house?"

"Only her." The EMT nodded at a woman standing nearby with hair as vibrant as the flames devouring the house. Another uniformed paramedic held one of her arms, while a firefighter stood in front of her, obviously blocking her path.

Gary rushed to the woman. "Ma'am? I'm Gary Anderson, acting sheriff. Will you come with me?"

Her green eyes flashed amid tears. "My house...my home."

He took her free elbow. "I understand, ma'am. Let's get your statement." He tugged gently, but she remained firm.

He nodded at the paramedic and together they turned her from the fire. "I really need to get your statement."

"We still need to take you to the hospital so they can check you out, ma'am," the EMT added.

They led her back to the emergency vehicle and helped her onto the stretcher inside. She sat with her gaze locked on the fire. Gary took a seat on the metal bench alongside her. He pulled out his notebook and pen, but didn't speak yet. He needed to observe both the scene and the victim first.

A purse lay on the floor beside the stretcher. He nudged it with his toe, questions flooding his mind. How had she managed to get her handbag out of the burning house, despite everything? Most people didn't think that clearly in a crisis of such magnitude. How had she?

"Did the firefighters pull her from the house?" he whispered to the paramedic.

"No. We found her in the driveway when we arrived." The EMT radioed Lagniappe Hospital.

Gary made a note, then turned his attention back to the woman sitting on the stretcher, her gaze locked onto the house now reduced to nothing more than a semblance of a bonfire.

The woman's copper-colored hair hung in big waves down her back, ending just below her shoulder blades. Soot stained her otherwise fair complexion. Wide eyes blinked from beneath almost invisible eyelashes. The plaid pajamas drooped off her slight frame. Gary took in how the hem hung well below her bare feet. Men's pajamas?

One of the paramedics held an oxygen mask to her face, while the other jumped from the back of the wagon and held the door. "You riding with us?"

Gary took another look at the woman and nodded. The doors slammed shut.

She shoved the mask aside. "Where are we going? I can't leave. My house." She grabbed an overhead rail and pulled herself to standing.

The EMT gently pushed her back down on the stretcher as the vehicle shifted into Drive. "We're taking you to the hospital for them to check you out."

She didn't appear pacified. Actually, irritation covered her delicate features.

"There's nothing you can do." Gary all but whispered the words, but they stopped her movements immediately.

Big tears fell from her eyes, making tracks down her cheeks through the soot.

"I'm sorry." And he truly was. He gripped his pen tighter. He hated this part of the job—having to ask questions and probe when people were hurting or grieving. But he'd never prove himself worthy of the chief deputy position if he didn't do what he must. He cleared his throat and took charge. "I need to know your name, ma'am."

"Monique. Monique Harris."

He wrote down her name, jotted his impressions of the scene, then met her stare. "Some of the questions I need to ask will be repeated by the fire chief, but it's just to make sure we cover everything, okay?"

She nodded as the paramedic shoved the oxygen mask back into her hands.

"Ms. Harris, did you leave a fire in the fireplace burning, something on the stove, anything like that?"

"No." She gulped in oxygen.

"Are you sure?"

She removed the mask from her face and glared at him. "I'm positive."

He made notes. "Have you recently had any electrical work done on the house?"

"No."

The vehicle hit a bump, jarring them. She swayed. He reached out and steadied her. Something zapped inside him. He jerked his hand back onto his lap. "Can you tell me what happened?"

"I was asleep. I guess the smoke woke me up." She worried her burned hands in her lap, not even realizing she cringed as she did. "I tried to get out the front door, but the fire was there. I went out the back door, the kitchen door. I-I…"

He touched her arm. "I understand. You got outside."

Tears streamed down her face. She was so small, so fragile. He had the strangest urge to pull her into his arms and pat her back, tell her everything would be okay. She looked so alone.

"Is there anyone I can call for you?"

She shook her head.

"A friend? Family member, maybe?"

"I have no one."

Poor thing, and now she'd lost her home, as well. Gary pushed down his empathy. Business. He had to do his job. Stay professional. He focused his attention on his notes and pressed on. "Do you have any idea what could have started the fire?"

Lifting her head, she set her chin. "Yes. Someone set this."

"You think this was deliberate? As in arson?" She was confused, obviously. Befuddled and distraught.

"I don't think, sir. I know." Her hands trembled as she ran her fingers through the tangle of hair.

"Ms. Harris, I'm sure you're very upset, but t—"

"Yes, I'm upset, but I'm not delusional. This was done deliberately."

He let out a soft sigh. Might as well humor her. "Okay, why would you think such a thing?"

"Because just this week I got a phone call telling me to leave."

TWO

She wasn't a pincushion! Monique scowled as the nurse finished taking blood.

The woman in blue scrubs stuck a Band-Aid over the site and patted Monique's shoulder. "The doctor will be with you in just a minute." She swished the curtain around the bed and disappeared.

The sounds of the emergency room were hushed, muffled. Phones rang and voices murmured.

Monique shifted, the bottoms of her feet throbbing. Wads of gauze coated her feet and hands. They'd treated her minor burns with ointment, but her hands were a different story. The mild burns from the floor were made worse from crawling over dirt and gravel. A good cause of possible infection, the triage nurse had admonished her. Like Monique had had another option? She tugged the warmed blanket up under her chin to fight off the chill. The nurse had warned her that feeling cold was to be expected.

She blinked back tears she refused to shed. She'd already cried enough. No, she wouldn't crumble—not now, not with all that she'd already survived. Yet her heart ached in a familiar way. How many times would she have to suffer because of the actions of another? Would she ever be able to live a normal life, without so much pain?

The curtain ripped away to reveal the man in uniform. Tall

and brawny with blond hair and soft blue eyes. "Hello, Ms. Harris. Remember me, Deputy Gary Anderson, acting sheriff of Vermilion Parish?"

She nodded and pushed into a sitting position, propping pillows behind her back. What now?

"The nurse said I could visit with you a few minutes until the doctor comes back. Is that okay with you?" His voice made her think he missed his calling—he should've been a radio deejay or a television anchor.

"Fine." He sure wasn't hard on the eyes, that much was certain. Monique chided herself and pulled the blanket higher as he shut the curtain and moved to stand alongside the bed. She shouldn't think such things about this man, or any man for that matter.

"Ms. Harris, I have a few more questions for you."

"Mrs."

"Excuse me?" He tilted his head, pen poised over his notebook.

"It's missus, not miss."

"Oh. My mistake. I apologize." He paused, tapping his pen against his chin. "Your husband's name?"

"Kent."

"I'm assuming he's out of town? Do you have a number so I can call and notify him? You'd probably like him to be here."

Tears stung her already worn-out eyes. "I'd love for him to be here, but he's dead." If only she could have him back for just one day, to feel his arms around her once again.

He paused. "I'm terribly sorry."

She sniffed and wiped her nose against the sleeve of her flannel pajamas. No, Kent's pajamas. The ones she wore on nights she missed him so much she ached with loneliness. Monique fought back new tears threatening to form. "Thank you."

When he didn't respond immediately, she lifted her gaze. His eyes were filled with such compassion, such pity. Just the things she'd fled Monroe to avoid. Her church family all treating her with kid gloves. The contacts at local businesses being overly polite and solicitous. It wasn't that she didn't appreciate their concern and caring, but everyone assumed she didn't want to talk about Kent and the life they'd shared. It was as if his murder had reached in and exposed an evil everyone chose to believe didn't exist in their tight-knit community.

Except for the police and the District Attorney's Office personnel. Those people wanted every detail she could ever recall. For the case. To catch and put away the man who'd murdered Kent in cold blood. She straightened against the flat pillows.

But she still didn't believe they'd accomplished their goal.

"How long ago?" The deputy's words were kind, his question not meant to be prying.

This lawman was different. She could detect his sympathy, but also something else. Something she couldn't identify, like a kinship of sorts. Which didn't exactly make a lick of sense, seeing as how she'd never met the man before in her life. "It'll be a year next month." The pain had only begun to diminish recently because of her excitement over beginning her new life. And now this had happened.

"I truly am sorry for your loss, Mrs. Harris."

"It's fine to call me Monique."

"Okay. Now, you told me that you received a phone call this week…?"

"Yes. I'd just returned home from the grocery store when the phone rang." She shivered, the room suddenly colder. "That surprised me because it'd only been turned on the day before."

"Can you remember what day that was exactly?"

"Um." She rewound her memory. Monday, she'd finished unpacking the rest of the dishes. Tuesday, she'd run into town to get her new cell phone and have her local phone service established because she figured everything would be closed on Thursday, New Year's Day. "Wednesday. New Year's Eve."

"Okay." He wrote in his notebook. "Go ahead."

"I answered. At first, no one said anything. I remember thinking it would be just my luck that the first phone call I received in my new house would be a wrong number." She fought to put a smile on her face but didn't quite make it. "So I repeated my hello again. I could hear someone breathing. Then all of a sudden, a man's voice told me *go home*. That's it—just two words. 'Go home.' Then he hung up."

"Did you recognize the voice?"

"No. I'm new here, haven't had a chance to meet anyone. Not even my neighbors." She gripped the edges of the blanket, twisting it into her fists and ignoring the pain. So much for fitting in, what she wanted more than anything else.

"Just the words *go home?* That was all he said?"

"Yep." She nodded for emphasis.

He rested the pen against the notebook and stared at her. "May I ask why you moved to Lagniappe?"

Wasn't *that* a loaded question?

She licked her cracked lips, then absentmindedly ran fingertips through her bangs. "Well, I recently discovered I have relatives living here."

"Recently discovered?" He arched a single brow.

"Yes." She knew how strange that sounded. Letting out a sigh, she decided to just spill the whole story. "I never knew who my father was. My mother refused to tell me, even when she was dying."

He scribbled in his notebook again.

"My husband was a private investigator, Deputy Anderson. When my mother passed away two years ago, I asked him to try to find out who my father was."

"And he did?"

"It took him some time, but yes, finally, he was successful." Monique closed her eyes as memories swarmed through her. "Right before Kent died, he obtained verified proof of who my father was." He'd been so excited to give her the news, had made a big deal out of delivering the information to her over a romantic dinner. He knew how much finding her family had meant to her, even as he knew she'd be upset to learn her father was a murderer. But at least she would know.

"And?"

She blinked open her eyes. "And I found out my father is incarcerated in the Oakdale, Louisiana, penitentiary for murder." She shivered, but not against the chilliness of the room this time. The irony staggered her—her biological father behind bars for killing a man, and her husband a murder victim. For the umpteenth time, her mind rallied. If she weren't so angry with God right now, she'd ask Him again why He'd allowed so much pain in her life. Then again, in the midst of the fire, she'd called out to Him. She'd have to analyze that later.

"What did you do?"

Monique focused on the lawman. "I went to visit him. To meet him. See him face-to-face."

Deputy Anderson waited.

"He denied I was his, even though I showed him the proof. I offered to undergo another DNA test for his own confirmation, but he refused." She trembled against the memory of how the denial had cut her to the quick. Right on the heels of losing Kent, her father's obvious displeasure at discovering he had a daughter had left her running out of the prison a simpering mess.

"Is the proof positive?"

"I think a DNA saliva test is pretty solid proof. They're ninety-eight percent accurate."

"How'd you get a sample of his saliva to run the test?"

She shifted. What did it matter? Kent was dead and couldn't get in trouble. "My husband arranged for one of the prison guards to get a sample of the man's saliva."

Deputy Anderson ducked his head and wrote. "I see."

No, he didn't. In her experience with police, they were all about black and white, no gray areas in anything. But what had been the harm in getting a saliva sample?

"What did you do after he denied being your father?"

Ouch. That stung. Monique released the blanket and sat straighter. "I used my husband's contacts to find out if he had any other children or relatives. Since my mother and Kent had died, I have no other family. I was curious." And desperately needing someone, something, to *belong* to.

"I can understand. Did you find a long-lost sibling?"

"No. As far as I can tell, my father had no other children. He never married, and he's seventy-four now." She smiled, despite her racing heart. "But I did find that he has a great-niece and a great-nephew."

"And they live here in Lagniappe?"

"Yes. And their mother, although they're related to my father on their paternal side."

"So, what are their names? Lagniappe's pretty small. I should know them."

Just what she was afraid of. She hadn't figured out yet how she'd approach them. What if they didn't want to get to know her? The second-guessing of her relocation hit her once again.

"Monique?"

She swallowed. "Luc and Felicia Trahan."

Luc and Felicia? Gary couldn't believe it. That would mean Monique's father was... "Justin Trahan is your biological father?"

"Does that surprise you?"

Well, not entirely. Justin, despite his advanced age, always did have a thing for the young ladies. But to have a daughter as young as her? "How old are you?"

"Twenty-six."

Just four years younger than he was.

Monique actually laughed. "I know, it was a shocker to me to see someone so much older than my mother. I'd expected someone in his fifties or so."

"Was your mother older when she had you?"

"Now, that's polite." She chuckled. "Not really. Mom was twenty-two when I was born. You do the math."

Gross. But he'd heard all the rumors about Justin. Still, it didn't make sense that Justin would deny being her father. Gary would think the man might like to have someone, anyone, visit him in jail. Felicia and Luc sure didn't. Not only had Justin killed their grandfather, Beau, his own brother, but he'd also confessed to killing their father years ago.

"Do you know them?"

Who in Lagniappe didn't? Luc and his wife, CoCo, were very popular. Luc played sax in a jazz band that performed regularly down at the club, while CoCo was Sheriff Theriot's sister-in-law. Felicia had married a local minister, Spencer Bertrand, and was the town darling. Everyone loved her.

"I do. They're wonderful people."

She sucked her bottom lip.

"What?"

"Do you think they'll want to meet me?" she asked.

"I don't know why not. Both of them are real good people. Neither are the least bit judgmental."

Monique's brows continued to scrunch.

"What's bothering you?"

She let out a long breath. "Well, I just had a thought."

"Which is?"

"What if they found out who I am and why I'm here? What if they don't want me around?"

Now he got where she was going. "You think one of them could've made that call to you?"

"It's possible, isn't it, Deputy?"

He laughed. Not just a chuckle but a full laugh. "If you knew them, you'd know how ridiculous that is. And if you think the caller also set your house on fire, well, I can tell you right now, that's not Luc or Felicia." Seeing her disbelieving expression, he fought to suppress his laughter. "Besides, Luc and his wife went out of town three days ago." CoCo's sister Tara was the sheriff's wife. Their other sister, Alyssa, had given birth to their first nephew, and CoCo, Luc, Bubba and Tara had all raced to New Orleans as soon as they'd gotten the call that Alyssa was in labor.

The doctor chose that moment to pull back the curtain. "I need to finish with my patient, Deputy."

"Sure." Gary nodded at Monique. "I'll just be in the waiting room." He strode down the hall to the area filled with uncomfortable chairs and the stench of burnt coffee.

Luc Trahan making anonymous, threatening phone calls? Felicia Trahan Bertrand? Just the notion of either of them doing anything like that made Gary laugh to himself. Ludicrous.

Needing fresh air, he stepped through the automatic double doors into the crisp night. He radioed an update to the dispatcher, then wondered how he'd get out of here. He'd ridden in the ambulance with Monique, leaving his cruiser at her place. Not that there would be much of a place now. He'd be surprised if anything remained after the fire.

Gary grabbed his cell phone from his belt clip, flipped it open and pressed the speed-dial number for his mother. He hated to wake her at this hour, but Deputy Marsh was off for the New Year's holiday, leaving only Deputy Mike Fontenot to cover the office. She answered without a trace of grogginess—probably up late working on those crossword puzzles she was addicted to. After asking her to come to the hospital to pick him up, it occurred to him that Monique had nowhere to go, and no way to get there. Knowing her sad recent past made him want to protect her even more. Especially in light of that phone call.

But about that menacing call…could she just be paranoid, making it up? He could certainly understand that, given how difficult this last year must've been for her. If she wasn't, then who called and threatened her? He shook his head. She sure seemed positive that someone had set her house on fire.

He had to admit, her story sounded plausible. From what he saw, the fire looked like it had been helped along. Accidental fires didn't burn that fast. If that was the case, it certainly brought on more questions.

Who didn't want her in Lagniappe? Who would be willing to turn to arson to get her to leave?

THREE

It looked like she was wearing fingerless gloves, like something out of the eighties.

Monique stared at her gauze-covered palms as she sat in the wheelchair waiting for the nurse to bring her discharge papers. She couldn't allow herself to wallow in self-pity. She wouldn't. She had to be strong, take charge. If she didn't, she'd crawl into a bed, pull the covers over her head and never emerge again.

She grabbed her purse from the foot of the ER bed, where the paramedic had placed it when he'd brought her in. At least she still had her cell phone and her wallet. Better call a cab to take her...where?

Despair circled her heart. Her home was gone—that much she could ascertain. Had she made a terrible mistake in selling her house and moving here? It'd been so hard to list the home she'd shared with Kent. But she'd needed a fresh start, a place to lick her wounds and build a new life. Start the New Year off in a new place. Lagniappe, where her relatives lived, had sounded like a good idea at the time. But now?

No, she wouldn't allow herself to be chased out of town. Not by threatening phone calls or even someone burning down her house. Kent had told her time and again that she was the strongest woman he knew. She wouldn't disappoint his memory of her inner strength. She'd find out who was behind all this, just as she'd been doing with his murderer. She'd see justice served, and this time, it would be total justice. Monique would do what she had to do.

And maybe find some sort of peace.

She fumbled in her purse for her cell. She'd have to find a hotel or motel and book a room. For an extended stay. She'd also have to buy clothes and toiletries. But right now, all she wanted to do was huddle under the covers and sleep. Her fingers grazed the worn pocket Bible Kent had loved so dearly. Fresh tears burned against her raw eyes.

So much for her inner strength and resolve.

"Mind if I disturb you again?" The deputy's smile was wide, engaging his entire face, as he stuck his head past the curtain.

"I'm really not up for more questions, Deputy. I'm tired, they gave me a shot of pain medication and I have to find someplace to stay for the night." She held up her phone to prove her claim.

"No more questions tonight, Mrs. Harris. I can finish my report tomorrow."

"Thank you." She ran her thumb over the raised buttons. "Could you possibly recommend a hotel or motel? One that's fairly close?"

Laughter flashed in his eyes. "Well, we only have one motel, and it's not even five minutes away."

Only one? "I wonder if they still have a room vacant."

He laughed aloud. "Are you kidding? They probably have all their rooms available. Lagniappe isn't exactly a tourist mecca."

Even being here only a week, she knew that. Or should've, if she'd been thinking clearly. "Oh. Well, guess I'd better call a cab." She paused, staring at him. "The town does have a taxi service, doesn't it?"

"We do, but I have a better idea. Why don't you let me take you to the motel?"

A lump lodged in her throat. She wasn't sure she was comfortable with that idea. Especially since she found him so unaccountably attractive. "I appreciate the thought, but I can call a cab. I don't want to be a bother."

"No bother. Hey, it reads on our cruisers 'to serve and protect.'" He winked. "Don't worry, I won't be driving."

She tilted her head against the pain medication beginning to take effect, making her feel as gauzy as the bandages on her hands and feet.

"I rode here with you, remember?"

"Oh. Right. So, how…?"

"My mother came to get me. She'd love to give you a ride."

His mother? Surely it'd be safe to let the nice lawman and his mother take her to the motel. Besides, she was so tired. Drained. And her mind just went totally blank.

"I promise we'll drive you straight to the motel, get you checked in and let you get some rest."

She offered a shaky smile. "Okay. Thank you."

"Good. I'll tell Mom to bring the car around." He left with a whoosh of the curtain.

Nice man. At least he seemed to be. Having spent time around the police during the investigation into Kent's murder, she knew not all cops were as nice and concerned. The lead detective in Kent's case had been more interested in getting a conviction and closing the case than in finding the truth.

She still didn't buy the murderer's testimony. Mainly that he drove the car *and* fired the gun that killed Kent. She was well trained and quite good with handguns. For a man high on drugs to fire a gun from the driver's seat, through the open passenger window of a moving car, and hit his target so accurately? It just didn't seem plausible to her. Hadn't back then, and didn't now.

"Here are your discharge papers and instructions." The nurse passed her several papers. "I just need your signature on the top copy."

Trying to sign her name using only the tips of her fingers was a challenge, but she managed to get a scrawl across the bottom of the form.

The nurse inspected it, nodded and passed her a little brown paper bag. "This is your antibiotic cream and gauze. I included several pairs of latex gloves to wear when you wash so you won't saturate your hands. I also put a couple of pairs of surgical booties in there. I'd suggest you wear them over the bandages on your feet when you bathe. And take baths, not showers. Prop your feet up so the bandages don't get wet. Change the dressings twice a day and if you see the wounds getting red or swollen, call us immediately."

Monique took the bag and set it in her lap. Not exactly the way she thought she'd be spending New Year's.

"Do you have someone coming to get you?" asked the nurse.

"Yes. He's having the car brought around." Whatever that meant.

"Good. Let me just wheel you out."

Nerves bunched in Monique's gut. She recognized it as coming down from an adrenaline rush. At times, she'd assisted Kent in his private-investigating business, and when they'd uncovered something vital, she'd experienced the adrenaline spike. She recognized the signs now—she'd crash soon.

A blast of cold air slammed into her as the double doors automatically whooshed open at the Emergency Room entrance. She shivered, missing the blanket she'd had to leave back in the examining area. With only flannel pajamas to protect her, Monique gripped her purse and paper bag tighter.

"What kind of car does he drive, honey?" The nurse engaged the locking mechanism on the wheelchair.

"Um…"

She was saved from having to respond by an older-model Ford sedan pulling up to the curb. Deputy Anderson jumped from the front seat on the passenger's side. "Sorry it took a minute. Mom had me clean out the backseat for you, so you could prop up your feet and all."

Monique smiled, grateful for the deputy and his mother.

He helped the nurse transfer Monique from the wheelchair into the car with her feet propped up on the worn vinyl, then returned to the passenger's seat. "Monique Harris, this is my mother, Della Anderson. Mom, this is Monique."

"Thank you so much for the ride, Mrs. Anderson."

"Oh, *ma chére,* it's Della. We're not too formal around here." The woman with eyes as soft as her son's slipped the car into gear and gunned the engine. "I'm just so sorry for what happened to you. I can't imagine. Must've been horrifying."

Monique smiled despite her exhaustion. It'd been a long time since someone had fussed over her so.

"Are those the only clothes you've got?" Della didn't wait for a reply before popping the deputy softly on the arm. "You need to get the girl some clothes. She can't run around in pajamas."

"Yes, ma'am." But he winked at Monique when his mother turned her attention back to the road.

"Crying shame, losing everything in a fire. I declare, it's a downright tragedy." Della glanced at Monique in her rearview mirror. "Don't you fret none, sweetie. I'll see that my boy gets you something to wear until you can go shopping."

They passed through downtown Lagniappe. Monique had been immediately attracted to its quaint charm. Didn't seem so quaint now, what with someone trying to run her out of town.

"Are you hungry? Would you like to get something to eat?"

Monique smiled at the woman's reflection. "No, ma'am. I'm just tired and want to get some sleep."

"Bless your heart. I understand. You'll be ready to eat in the morning." Della tossed her son a knowing look.

Grinning at their interplay, Monique leaned her head against the seat and closed her eyes. Fatigue overcame every muscle in her body.

The car came to a stop.

Monique opened her eyes and sat straight. They were parked outside the front office of the Lagniappe Motel. Deputy Anderson climbed out of the car. "I'll be right back."

She shifted her purse and bag. Oh, no. She'd forgotten to give him money to pay for the room. Well, he was the town deputy, after all. He'd probably tell them she'd settle up in the morning. Monique hid a yawn behind her hand.

He returned, brandishing a key. "Pull up there, Mom." He nodded toward the room closest to the office. "I asked that you be given a room up front. Just in case you needed anything."

"Thanks." She hid another yawn.

Quicker than she thought would be possible, he'd opened the motel room door for her, helped her inside and promised to come check on her in the morning and finish taking her statement. He took her cell number, gave her his, then he was gone.

Alone in the motel room, Monique hobbled toward the bed. So, so tired. She set her purse on the nightstand, grabbed the bag and tottered to the bathroom. At the sink, she bent to rinse out her mouth. Her hair fanned her face, and the smell of smoke overtook her. She almost retched. No, she couldn't go to sleep yet. She needed to bathe and wash her hair. But she'd make it quick.

She opened the paper bag and withdrew the gloves and surgical booties, then caught her reflection. She looked awful. Like something the cat drug up. But her eyes were the worst. Oh, not from the smoke and fire. Her eyes looked haunted, as if she'd seen too much for them to take.

Technically, she had.

She crumbled to the floor and let the sobs overtake her. Despite her resolution to stay strong, it was all too much. So she gave in to the tears. Tears of grief over losing Kent, tears of pain, and tears of frustration that she seemed helpless to stop the hurricane her life had become.

Saturday morning dawned bright and beautiful with the sun slipping through the live oaks surrounding the bayou. Gary took a sip of coffee as he stood on the balcony of his apartment. Even though he hadn't hit the hay until well after one in the morning, his internal clock had awoken him at six sharp. Now, a shower and two hours later, he readied for work.

His cell phone chirped.

Very few people called him so early, especially on the weekend. Had to be work. He snatched the phone from the dinette table. "Anderson."

"Good morning. Glad I caught you before you left. I called the ladies at church and rounded up some clothes for Monique. She can't go shopping in pajamas, for goodness' sake. And I've just put in a pan of biscuits and I'm making the sausage gravy now. You come on and swing by here for the clothes, and I'll have a plate ready for you to take to her."

Gary couldn't help smiling. His mother, though never having much herself, always thought of other people's needs. No one could ever say Della Anderson wasn't a generous and giving woman. "Yes, ma'am. I'll be there inside of twenty minutes."

He dressed in his uniform straight from the dry cleaners and headed to the cruiser. After they'd dropped Monique off at the motel last night, his mother had taken him to get the car. And they'd seen the damage left by the fire.

It wasn't pretty.

The porcelain bathtub was the only thing left standing. That, and a portion of the toilet. An SUV had been parked under one of the oak trees kitty-corner to the house. It'd been saved from the fire, luckily. The air breezing over the bayou had been filled with the stench of burning wood. His mother had felt even more for Monique after seeing the total devastation.

Della met him at the door. "What took you so long? The gravy's gonna get thick." She presented her cheek for a peck.

Gary obliged, kissing her softly.

"Take those bags out to your car while I fix her plate." She nodded to three paper sacks sitting by the door.

"Um, don't I get a plate?" he teased.

His mother smiled and swatted him with a hand towel. "I'm making two plates for y'all. Figured you could eat with her and see how she's getting on."

He lifted the sacks with a grin and carried them to his car. Once he returned, his mother met him with two big containers as well as a thermos. "Two biscuits and gravy plates and some good coffee."

"Thanks, Mom." He took the offering and planted another kiss on her temple. "You're the best."

She blushed and shooed him away.

After settling the containers on the passenger's seat, he steered the cruiser toward the motel. How was the lovely Monique Harris going to feel about him showing up at eight o'clock on Saturday morning to share breakfast with her? Too late to back out now. His mother would no doubt seek Monique out and ask her about the food and clothes. She'd be crushed if he didn't deliver the goods.

No cars were at the motel, save the office clerk's little hatchback. Gary parked in front of Monique's room, praying she wasn't still sleeping. Juggling the containers and thermos, he knocked softly on the door.

Long seconds passed. Maybe she was still asleep.

The door inched open. Monique's wide eyes peered from the crack.

"Good morning. Breakfast is served, courtesy of my mother, who, by the way, is one of the best cooks in the parish." He held up the thermos. "And coffee comes with it." He couldn't believe that his nerves were as knotted as a cypress tree. Sure, he'd never been a Casanova around the ladies, but something about Monique Harris made him feel like an awkward schoolboy.

She hesitated only a moment before opening the door. When she smiled at him, his heart stuttered for a moment. He forced himself to calm down. She was a subject, nothing more. He had too much to lose if he didn't stay on top of his game. That was his only interest in her—solving her case.

"Thank you. I appreciate it. I was wondering how I was going to go out for something to eat in my pajamas." She took the thermos and set it on the little table by the window. "I didn't think the motel would have room service."

He chuckled, admiring her sense of humor when he knew she had to be devastated. "And there's more. Mom gathered some clothes for you. Probably nothing worthy of a fashion magazine, but it'll be something to hold you over until you can go shopping." He headed back to the car to grab the sacks when a thought hit him. What if she didn't have any money to buy clothes and other necessities? She'd just bought a house.

"Oh, my." Monique took one of the sacks from him and set it on the foot of the bed. "Wow. This is too much. Your mother didn't have to do all this."

Heat crept up his neck. Was she insulted? "That's just the way Mom is, always wanting to help. She doesn't mean anything by it." He set the remaining bags beside the other and took a seat in one of the two chairs by the little table.

Monique tossed him a funny look, much like the one his mother sent him when he'd fidgeted too much in church, and glanced inside the sack. "This is wonderful. I'm very grateful. I didn't have a clue how I was going to be able to get out and buy anything."

"Great. Let's eat." He put one of the containers in front of the vacant chairs.

She stopped. "Oh. That's right, you need to finish questioning me." She hobbled to the chair and plopped down, pulling the cheap motel blanket around her.

"We don't have to do that just yet." He opened the thermos and filled the two plastic motel cups with strong coffee. "Why don't we just eat for now? We'll need to make arrangements for you to get your vehicle."

"If it wasn't damaged by the fire. I can't remember how close I parked to the house." She shook her head. "And I'd just gotten that SUV before I moved here. Traded in my old hatchback."

"It looks fine."

She caught his gaze over the table.

Her wide-eyed stare kicked him in the gut. If he did his job as he should, he'd be able to help this poor woman. And that's all he needed to worry about—doing his job. He cleared his throat. "I had to get my car last night, remember?"

"Right." She opened the lid off the container. "Wow, this is a lot of food."

"Mom believes in never leaving a table hungry." He chuckled.

She joined in his laughter. "I can see that."

"Would you like to offer grace?"

Monique froze, fork midair. "Um, you go ahead."

His heart fell. She wasn't a believer. He ducked his head, offered a prayer and then met her gaze again.

"Sorry. It's just that after what happened with Kent, God and I aren't exactly on speaking terms right now."

"I see."

But he didn't. In the roughest times of his life, his faith had often been the only thing that got him through. If Monique couldn't turn to God now when she'd lost everything else, she truly was lost herself.

Dear Lord, please use me to minister to her. Guide me to be Your witness in her life right now.

FOUR

"Can you think of any reason why someone would want to scare you out of town?"

Saturday breakfast was officially over. The deputy sat with his notebook open, pen poised and inquiring stare locked directly on Monique's face. He looked very handsome with that serious expression on his face. Even with her clogged sinuses, she could detect the hint of his aftershave. Woodsy and nature-y. And surprisingly comforting.

"I told you yesterday, maybe my new relatives found out who I am and that I'm in town and didn't like it." She lifted what she hoped looked like a casual shoulder.

He shook his head. "I can't believe Luc or Felicia would do such a thing."

"You won't even talk to them about this?" Monroe, Louisiana, wasn't exactly a metropolis, but at least they followed through on leads. In contrast, this small town policing left a lot to be desired. What had she gotten into by coming here?

"Sure, I'll talk to them, but I'm almost positive they aren't involved. Probably don't even know you exist. I'm asking if you can think of anyone else."

Great. He'd *talk* to them. She could only imagine how that questioning would play out.

"Is there someone in your life from Monroe who could be threatening you?"

"The accomplice to my husband's murder."

The pen dropped from his fingers to roll on the table. "Your husband was murdered?"

Time for the whole story now. She'd hoped not to have to tell this tale yet again, but knew that was just wishful thinking. Her mouth went dry. She took a sip of the now-cooled coffee. "Yes. Killed in a drive-by shooting."

His eyes softened with his tone. "Would you mind elaborating, if you can?"

"Kent was a private investigator, one of the best in the parish. He'd even been hired a couple of times by the Monroe Police Department to work a cold case when they had nothing. He was that good." Tears burned in her throat. When would she be able to tell the story without having her heart ripped from her chest? Maybe when she felt justice had been served. Real justice.

Gary laid his hand over hers. "I don't mean to pry. I'm just trying to do my job and figure out what's going on. Do my best to keep you safe."

"It's okay." She pulled her hand into her lap. "He was leaving work one night and was shot and killed."

"Is that common in Monroe?"

She forced a weak smile. "Not so much."

"Did the police ever catch the shooter?"

She nodded. "Someone's in prison for murdering Kent, yes."

"But? I detect a bit of hesitation there."

Pausing, she inhaled and exhaled slowly. "I think he had an accomplice who was never charged. I think one guy took the fall."

"Why?"

"Because the guy in jail confessed to being both the driver and the shooter. His prints were on the gun, his hand had gunpowder residue."

"Did he admit to having an accomplice?"

"No. He testified that he acted alone."

"You don't buy it?"

"The driver and the shooter being the same person? No, I don't think so."

"Why would he confess to acting alone? Protecting someone, maybe?"

"I don't know. I begged the Monroe Police Department to look into that angle, but they didn't bother."

"What was the reason he gave for shooting your husband?"

She swallowed against the lump in her throat. "He said it was random, that he didn't even know who Kent was. He claimed he was high."

"Did the tox screens confirm that?"

"Yes, but he was always high. A lot of drug usage in his history. Coke, meth, pot, pills…you name it, this guy had tried it."

"But you don't believe he acted alone?"

"Not for one minute. It's too tidy." She ran her finger around the rim of the plastic cup. "You're a cop—you tell me, how convenient is it that he hadn't gotten rid of the gun he shot Kent with, didn't even bother to wipe his prints off it and that he was caught before he took a shower and washed away the gunpowder?" She tossed her hair over her shoulder. "It smacks of having a patsy so the police wouldn't look any further."

"If he was high then mayb—"

She shook her head. "You know better. Those guys—the ones who do drugs daily, the career criminals—they know how to cover their tracks. Why didn't he? And why'd he confess so quickly? According to the detectives, they didn't have a single clue before an anonymous tip led them straight to this guy."

"Why would this guy take the full heat? Confess to acting alone?"

Exactly. "That's what I hounded the police to ask themselves."

"And?"

"And they told me that sometimes bad things happen to good people. End of story. Case closed. They never even uncovered who that anonymous tipster was."

He rolled the pen between his forefinger and thumb. "So why would someone tied into your husband's murder threaten you here? How do you figure a connection?"

"Maybe because they know I'm not going to give up on finding everyone involved in Kent's death. I won't stop until I get to the truth." Her heart raced. She couldn't. She owed it to Kent. And herself. "I just needed to take a break from everything. Clear my head."

"That still has no bearing on you being in Lagniappe."

He had a point. "No, but I can't think of anyone else who would want me to leave. I just got here. Maybe they're trying to scare me—period. Or distract me from the truth so I don't think it's connected."

"Have you spoken to anyone here? Someone who maybe acted strangely toward you?"

"No." She rubbed her thumb against the bandages on her hand. "But it could be linked to Kent's murder. They'll do anything to make me stop, even burning down my house with me inside."

"We don't know the cause of the fire yet."

She did. "I smelled something strange. I know it was set, I know it."

"We'll have to wait for the official report before we can treat it as arson. Until then, I need to ask you a few more questions."

Didn't the police always have a *few more questions?* "Of course."

"Walk me through what you did last night before retiring."

She picked at the gauze on her hands. "I grabbed a peanut-butter-and-jelly sandwich for supper, so I know nothing was left on in the kitchen. I haven't used the stove or oven at all since moving in." She met his stare with a tilt of her chin. No way were they going to tell her the fire was a result of her actions.

"Then what?"

"I cleaned up the kitchen and took a shower."

"That would be in the master bathroom?"

"Yes." No, she'd walked up the stairs and used the bathroom there. What kind of question was that?

"And after your shower?"

"I crawled into bed and went to sleep."

He scratched notes. "And you heard nothing? Saw nothing until you were awakened?"

"Nothing." She shook her head. If only she *had* seen or heard something. "I woke up to the smell of smoke and the sound of crackling." Monique shivered. She'd never forget those sounds for as long as she lived. They'd haunt her dreams.

"About what time did you go to bed?"

She let out a deep breath, trying to recall. "Best guess would be around ten-ish. I was tired, really exhausted, and just wanted to get a good night's rest."

He nodded as he wrote. "I'll get the time the 9-1-1 call came into dispatch." He set down the pen and met her gaze. "Anything else you can think of? Even something minor you think doesn't matter. It could be important."

As if she hadn't been told the same thing before? The investigators handling Kent's murder had drilled that line into her head over and over again, like a mantra. "I can't think of anything else."

He stood, shutting his notebook and slipping it into his shirt pocket. "Why don't I let you get ready and then I'll take you to get your car?"

"Sounds good." She stood, balancing on her tiptoes to avoid putting pressure on her feet. The pain medication from the night before had long worn off, and she'd forgotten to take a pill this morning. "It shouldn't take me longer than thirty or forty minutes to get ready."

"No rush. I've got a couple of things to do. I'll just pick you up in an hour."

She saw him out, then leaned her back against the closed motel door. Did he believe her? He hadn't seemed eager to entertain the notion of someone setting her house on fire. But she knew the truth. That call had been a warning. Now she knew someone didn't want her in town and they were serious.

Even if the police blew her off, she'd figure out on her own who was behind the threat and the fire. And why they didn't want her in Lagniappe.

Why would someone try to run Monique Harris out of town?

Gary sat in the cruiser, reviewing his notes. He'd have to make a full report sometime today, but he didn't want to slant it toward arson if there was a logical reason her house had caught fire. And he didn't want to mention the threatening phone call if Monique had fabricated the whole thing.

His gut told him that despite the ordeal and the trauma she'd undergone in the last year, Monique Harris wasn't melodramatic or delusional. She seemed levelheaded and calm, even when listing her reasons to believe someone was after her, with no proof.

She was also very attractive. The type of woman who was both strong and vulnerable at the same time, making him want to protect and stand beside her. His mother had seen it, too. Still, she was a subject in an ongoing investigation. He was the lead officer. To be considered for chief deputy, he'd have to handle this case with kid gloves—do everything by the book, dotting each *i* and crossing each *t*. And not noticing things like just how pretty she looked in the morning sunlight.

His cell phone trilled.

He flipped it open. "Anderson."

"Yes, son, I know your name. I gave birth to you, remember?"

Gary smiled at his mother's teasing. "Your biscuits and gravy were a hit. So were the clothes."

"Oh, good. I wanted to check on that poor girl. How is she?"

Beautiful? Admirable? "She's getting ready now, then I'll take her to get her car."

"Gary Anderson, you aren't in that motel room while she's getting ready, are you? What will people say? If you aren't considering your reputation, think about that poor girl's."

He chuckled. "Mom, I'm sitting in my car outside the motel, doing some paperwork."

"Well, good thing. That poor child doesn't need anything else poured on top of her. She just lost everything she has."

"Don't worry about it. You raised me better than that."

"I'd hope so."

He swallowed another laugh. "I need to finish up some stuff before she comes out. I'll call you later."

"Why don't you invite her to join us for supper tonight?"

"Mom, I already told you that I won't be able to come over this week. Not with the sheriff on vacation."

"But that young lady needs some TLC. Surely you can manage for supper? Where's your compassion? It's the Christian thing to do."

But would doing so put him in an awkward position with respect to the case? He couldn't afford to cause any raised eyebrows. "I'll see what I can do and let you know."

"By noon, son, so I know how much to cook."

As if his mother ever cooked less than enough to feed an army. "Love you."

He closed the phone and dropped it into the console, then went back to his thoughts on Monique's allegations. No, Monique wasn't a crackpot. She'd endured a very hard and trying situation, but she wasn't a loon.

First things first, though. He'd call Felicia Trahan Bertrand and see if she even knew about Monique's connection to Justin Trahan. Monique's accusing Felicia or Luc of making the threatening phone call still made him chuckle. Once she met them, she'd see how outlandish the notion was herself.

The police radio squawked to life. "Deputy Anderson, come in."

He smiled at the dispatcher's twang as he lifted his mic. "Go ahead, Missy."

"Need you back at the station. Fire chief's here, needing to talk to you pronto."

Gary glanced at his watch, then back at the motel door. Forty minutes remained on the hour he'd given Monique. "Roger that. On my way."

He put the car in gear and steered toward the sheriff's station. No traffic slowed the straight shot into downtown. He parked in the sheriff's space and sauntered into the station, heading back to the sheriff's office.

The older man stood just inside the office. "Deputy Anderson."

Gary moved past him and sat behind the desk, waving him to the chairs. The faint remnants of smoke and ash clogged the air surrounding the fire chief. Gary cleared his throat. "Thanks for coming by."

The man shook his head. "No problem. Just wanted to let you know that we've determined the fire was arson. A form of diesel fuel was used as the accelerant."

So Monique had been right. "Any clues?"

"Not yet. We've called in the arson investigation unit. They'll send an investigator down this way tomorrow. We'll know more once he gets here and does his initial walk-through."

Gary stood and offered his hand. "I appreciate the heads-up."

The older man shuffled from the office, leaving Gary alone with his thoughts. Again his logic and emotions were at war. On the one hand, he had the utmost sympathy and compassion for Monique and what she'd endured and would have to continue to face in the coming weeks and months. But on the flip side, excitement filled him. A real case. One that needed solving. And if he managed to pull that off before the sheriff returned, he'd be a shoe-in for the chief deputy position. Add to that the concern for Monique. Now there was proof positive her house had been burned down on purpose. What if someone was intent on finishing the job they'd started? Was it just a scare tactic, or was Monique really in danger?

But it wasn't just that he felt he'd earned the promotion. No, the new position also came with a raise. With the extra money, he could do more for his mother. Buy her some of the nice things she'd never had. With all the sacrifices she'd made for him over the years, he wanted to make her life easier, help her out more financially.

The minutes ticked by as he weighed his dilemma. He prayed for guidance, then pushed to his feet. He needed to get back to the motel to pick up Monique.

She was standing in the doorway when he pulled into the parking lot. Decked out in a pair of sweatpants and a T-shirt of his mother's, she looked barely eighteen. The urge to protect and shield her sparked in him again. Especially when she smiled at him as she hobbled to the car.

He jumped out and opened the passenger door for her, then shut it firmly after she was tucked safely inside.

"I really appreciate the ride. I called the front desk and booked the room for a couple of weeks. I need to call my insurance company Monday. I don't suppose they're open on Sunday." She let out a heavy sigh. "So much to do that I almost don't know where to start."

He turned the car toward her place. "Monique, the fire chief has made his preliminary report."

"And?"

"Arson."

"I knew it." She nodded, but more to herself than him.

"They've called in an arson investigator."

"Good. I'll need to let my insurance company know."

Did she realize she'd be the first person they looked into? With arson, they always investigated the person who owned the property, who stood to gain from a loss. Especially when it was heavily insured. Did she have a big policy? "Who's your insurance with?"

"Bayou Insurance." She let out a chuckle, and his heart skipped. Throaty and deep, her laugh did strange things to his insides. "Isn't that just a fitting name?"

He filed away the information and joined her chuckle. "I guess so."

"So, I'm going to have to look for a rental or something until I can find another place to buy. Know any good rentals?"

"You aren't going to pack it up and go home?"

She cocked her head. "And let someone run me off with my tail between my legs? Not hardly. I've had quite enough of other people wreaking havoc in my life, thank you very much. I won't let myself become a victim again. Besides, I sold my house in Monroe—I have no family there. This is my home now."

She exuded a quiet strength, one he had to respect. If only she didn't look so young and exposed. "Sure, I can recommend a couple of rental places."

"I'd appreciate that."

He steered the car into her driveway and felt rather than heard her gasp. She opened the door as soon as the cruiser came to a stop.

"Oh, my."

The air still reeked of smoke, but at least his eyes didn't burn. He followed her toward her car, holding her elbow as she picked her way over the rocks and loose gravel.

She stared at the still smoldering embers that had once been her home. "There's nothing to salvage." She swallowed hard. "Everything's gone. My wedding album, the china Kent and I got for a wedding present... It's almost as if my life is slowly being erased."

"I'm sorry." And he truly was.

She met his stare. "I'll find out who did this, and see justice served."

Her tone left no question as to whether or not she was serious. "This is a police matter now. You need to let us handle it."

She turned her gaze back to the rubble, and didn't reply.

FIVE

Why was she so nervous?

Monique fumbled with the buttons to the dress she'd bought yesterday. Her hands felt better, to the point where she hadn't needed as much gauze this morning. Her feet, however, were still an issue. No way would she be able to wear dress shoes to church this morning. She'd have to make do with the slip-on Crocs Ms. Della had given her.

Studying her reflection in the mirror, she again questioned her nervousness. Going to a new church for the first time always put people a bit on edge. But it was more than that for Monique. She hadn't darkened the door of a sanctuary since Kent's funeral. And today her reasons for attending weren't to mend the rift between her and God, although she knew she'd have to deal with that relationship later. Today, her main reason—her only reason, to be honest—was to check out Felicia Trahan Bertrand, the pastor's wife and Monique's cousin.

She couldn't depend on Gary Anderson to adequately question Felicia about the menacing phone call. His entire attitude whenever she suggested either of her cousins could be involved in the call or the arson was laughable. He simply didn't take the possibility seriously. Sure, the woman was a pastor's wife, but in Monique's experience from assisting Kent in his private investigation business, no one—not preachers nor their wives—

was above suspicion. Determination to uncover the truth drove her to finish dressing and flip off the bathroom light.

No more procrastination. She grabbed her purse and keys, secured the motel room door, and shuffled to her SUV. The nice desk clerk had given her instructions to Pastor Bertrand's church just outside Lagniappe's city limits.

The sun shone brightly over the bayou and little sunbeams danced on the cracked windshield of her Expedition. She shook her head. The cracks hadn't been there before—the heat from the fire must have caused them. Just something else she'd have to handle.

She pulled into the packed parking lot of the church. Didn't anyone attend the church in Lagniappe? She hadn't expected this many cars. How would she be able to pick out her cousin and study her?

With great hesitation, Monique made her way toward the timeworn church sitting on the edge of the bayou. A burst of wind skimmed over the water, carrying a fishy odor on its wings. Monique crinkled her nose and gripped the handrail. The last thing she needed was to draw attention to herself by falling down the steps. Nope, that wouldn't be good at all.

A man not much older than she, with shaggy hair and a big grin, held out his hand. "Good morning."

"Morning." Her voice was barely over a whisper. What was wrong with her? The butterflies in her stomach refused to be still.

"I'm Spencer Bertrand." He took her elbow and helped her up the last stair, glancing at her hands but politely making no mention of the gauze.

Her cousin's husband, in the flesh. "I-I'm Monique. Monique Harris."

"Are you visiting the area?" His eyes were soft, caring, like a preacher's should be.

She licked her chapped lips. "I just moved to Lagniappe."

"Then, welcome." He opened the door to the sanctuary for her before turning to greet the next group of people making their way up the stairs.

Monique let out a slow breath as she stepped into the entryway. The sanctuary loomed before her like a hungry, gaping mouth. She shivered and knew it had nothing to do with the crisp January morning.

Music surrounded her as she walked down the well-traveled carpet, trying to spot a vacant pew somewhere near the back. She wanted to be able to watch, see if she could spot her cousin, the preacher's wife. As she eased into an aisle seat, the bass reverberated in her chest so that she actually *felt* the worship song.

All around her, people whispered or greeted one another. Some stood and sang along with the music. The old familiar peace beckoned to her, calling into the deepest part of her soul. Uninvited tears filled her eyes. She blinked and shook her head, not ready to let go of her anger, her outrage. Her fear.

A young woman with honey-colored hair walked up the center aisle, stopping at each pew to speak to someone. Monique couldn't take her eyes off the woman. Although a noticeable limp marred her movement, there was a quiet grace about her. An ethereal glow flowed from her.

She smiled at Monique and moved toward her, hand outstretched. "Hello. Welcome to the church."

Monique touched the woman's hand with the tips of her fingers. "Thank you."

"I'm Felicia Bertrand."

Freezing, Monique struggled to form her own name. This was her cousin! "I'm M-Monique Harris."

Felicia's smile widened. "I'm glad you're here to worship with us this morning, Monique."

"Thank you." Monique ducked her head.

"Well, *bonjour,* Gary."

Felicia's cheerful greeting brought Monique's head up with a snap. Sure enough, Deputy Gary Anderson stood in the aisle, grinning at Felicia as if she'd hung the moon. In a pair of jeans and a sweater, he looked much more masculine than in that silly deputy sheriff uniform. She stopped her thoughts right there. No, she couldn't notice how the navy sweater set off his Caribbean-blue eyes.

The warmth in those eyes was brighter than the overhead lights of the sanctuary. "Good morning, Felicia. How are you?"

"Fine. Where's Ms. Della?"

"She's attending services in Lagniappe today. You know how she likes to support both churches."

Felicia laughed. "That she does, and she does it so well. You be sure to tell her I said hello and expect to see her here next Sunday, yes?"

"I'll do that." Gary's hand found its way to Monique's shoulder. "I see you've met Monique."

Dread of what he'd say next had Monique fighting the urge to throttle his outspoken self. The pain and gauze were the only things that stopped her. Was he here to protect her, or Felicia? Did he think she'd just openly accuse her cousin, right here in the middle of church? She shrugged off his touch.

Felicia glanced from Monique to Gary. "You two know each other?"

"Yes. Monique's house burned down Friday night."

"Oh, I'm so sorry." Felicia stared at Monique with nothing but compassion blinking in her eyes. "I didn't know. I'd heard about the fire, of course, but had no idea anyone was living there. You bought the old Pittman place?"

"So I've been told." Monique studied the other woman intently. No shocked expression. No changing the subject. Nothing to indicate any knowledge or involvement.

"Is there anything I can do for you?"

Confess to putting someone up to calling and threatening me? "No. No, thank you." Somewhere in her heart, she already knew Felicia had nothing to do with that ominous call or the fire. The deputy had been right.

And that irritated her all the more.

"You must come to my house after church, yes? Spence and I always have a small gathering for lunch. Today it'll just be my mother since my brother and sister-in-law are out of town. Say you'll come." She touched Gary's shoulder. "You, too, of course."

He laughed and rubbed his stomach. "I never turn down an opportunity to sample your cooking, Felicia."

She chuckled and shook her head before winking at Monique. "Men. All they think about is food, yes? So, please say you'll come. I'd love to get to know you a little bit. Nothing overbearing. I promise."

How could Monique resist this gentle woman? "Uh, okay. If I can find your house. You'll have to give me directions."

The preacher chose that moment to take to the podium. Felicia straightened.

"Don't worry about it. I'll make sure she gets there." Gary stepped across Monique to sit beside her.

"Great. See you both later." Felicia turned and made her way to the front pew.

Monique stiffened as the call to worship began. She stood when everyone else did.

"You're welcome," Gary whispered in her ear.

Oh, she really did want to throttle him.

Monique sat right next to him, but it felt like she was a million miles away.

Gary shifted on the pew again, awaiting Pastor Bertrand's closing prayer. He cut his eyes to the woman beside him. Monique hadn't so much as breathed in his direction since the service started. She'd inched away from him, practically hugging the edge of the pew, making sure her shoulder didn't even graze his.

He didn't understand the animosity radiating from her. He hadn't spilled the beans about who she was and why she'd come to Lagniappe. He'd been nice and cordial. What was her problem?

Maybe she was uncomfortable because she was in church

when she'd told him she wasn't on speaking terms with God. Maybe her demeanor had nothing to do with him.

He'd had the intention of staying away from Monique, of keeping everything professional, yet he'd agreed to join her at the Bertrands'? No, that was business. He'd observe the way Felicia reacted when Monique told her of their relations. For his report only, of course.

She finally glanced at him. He smiled. She sent him a glare that could melt the wax off the altar candles.

Nope, her manner had everything to do with him.

The opening bars of the closing hymn filled the sanctuary, the words of praise settling over him like a salve. He ignored the woman beside him, stood and lifted his voice with the rest of the congregation. No way would he allow anybody, not even a beautiful, intriguing woman, to come between him and worship. Besides, Monique was nothing more to him than the subject in his case, right? Right.

Before the last strand of music died away, Monique hopped out of her seat and hobbled toward the entrance of the church. Gary nodded at friends as he made his way to the door. He slowed his pace when he saw that Pastor Spence had engaged Monique in a conversation of sorts. Smiling, he moved behind her.

"Felicia tells me you'll be joining us for lunch. I'm so happy you're coming," Pastor Spence said.

"Hope you don't mind—Felicia invited me, as well." He offered his hand to the preacher. "Great sermon today."

"Thanks. Yep, she told me. The more the merrier." Pastor Spence smiled back at Monique. "Do you know how to get to the house?"

"I'll make sure she gets there okay." Gary put his hand on her shoulder.

She jerked away from his touch and glared at him.

Spence threw him a confused look, to which Gary only shrugged. "Uh, well, good," Spence said. "Okay, I'll see y'all shortly."

Monique pushed out the door and walked down the stairs, her

escape hampered by her injuries. Gary paced himself alongside her. "Have I done something to offend you?"

She stopped and stared at him, those wide green eyes of hers flashing with anger or annoyance, he couldn't tell which. "Did it ever occur to you that I don't need someone to speak for me? That I'm perfectly capable of introducing myself to my relatives all by myself? That maybe I didn't want her to know about my house burning down just yet? Maybe I wanted to tell her who I was first. Did you ever think about that?"

He shook his head. She wasn't making a lick of sense. "I didn't tell her you're related to her, and if you think it's a secret your house burned down, think again. Small towns thrive on gossip." Gary struggled to keep his tone light, refusing to match her snippy tone. "Besides, you're the one who wants me to question her and Luc about the warning call."

"But I wanted to tell her in my way, in my time. She didn't know it was my house that burned, which indicates you hadn't talked to her yet. You aren't taking me seriously."

She had a point. He'd intended to call Felicia and question her, but he'd just been busy with other things. Regret moved around his spine like kudzu. "Look, I'm sorry if I overstepped any bounds. I was only trying to help you."

"I wanted to do this myself," she said more to herself than to him.

"If you don't want me to go to lunch, I'll just give you directions."

Jutting out her chin in that cute, defiant way of hers, Monique paused for a long moment. "She invited you."

"So she did, but I can always cancel if you'd prefer to go alone."

Time stretched between them. Members of the congregation called out greetings to him as they crossed the parking lot. Car doors slammed. Kids laughed, their feet clomping against pavement. The sun warmed the breeze swirling around the gravestones in the adjacent cemetery.

"No. I'm sorry. I shouldn't have acted like that." With a contriteness in her tone, Monique lowered her head. "I really am sorry. It's just that I was nervous and uncomfortable to begin with, and I'm working on being totally independent."

She lifted her head. Moisture had pooled in her eyes. "Ever since Kent died, I've wanted to be able to stand on my own, but every time I turn around, I can't. Something happens that makes me feel helpless again. I'm so tired of having other people's actions dictate what I do."

He swallowed the truth, knowing she wasn't ready to hear that God would continue to cause things to happen that required her to seek out help. It was a visible sign that Father was calling her back into the fold.

"No worries. So, shall we go to the Bertrands'?" He glanced over his shoulder. "The lot's about clear, so it won't be long until Felicia and Spence head home."

"Oh. I need to go back to the motel and change first."

"Why don't I pick you up there, and you can ride with me?"

A cloud covered her face. "I don't need a babysitter."

She sure was oversensitive. Gary reminded himself that she had just endured a very trying experience on the tail of another one. Maybe he should cut her some slack. "I don't think you do. Just trying to be a nice guy."

"I'm sorry. Man, I keep having to apologize. I'm normally not this snarky."

"It's okay. You've been through a lot."

She smiled, warming him more than the sunshine bearing down upon them. "Thank you for being so understanding." She hitched her purse strap up on her shoulder. "I'd very much appreciate you picking me up for lunch. Thank you."

"Great. I'll pick you up in, say, half an hour?"

"Perfect."

He shut her truck door for her, his mind reeling as he walked to the cruiser. Glancing at the cell phone in the console, he noticed that he had missed calls and voice mail. He flipped open the phone and dialed into his messages.

The first one was his mother, asking him to invite Monique over for lunch.

The next message was from the weekend dispatcher, notifying him the arson investigator, a Mr. Bob Costigan, had arrived in town, and was in the Lagniappe Motel and would await Gary's call.

Interesting. They sure had moved fast in getting the investigator to town.

He called his mother, told her there was no way he could make lunch, then ended the call. His mind went to the other message. About the arson investigator.

Things could get very interesting with Mr. Costigan and Monique both staying at the only motel in Lagniappe. Yep, sparks could definitely fly, depending on how Mr. Costigan's investigation proceeded.

SIX

The woman was too good to be true.

Monique stared at Felicia as the preacher's wife set the table. "Are you sure I can't help you?"

The kitchen smelled of spices and aromas that made Monique's mouth water. Gary hadn't been kidding about Felicia's cooking, if the smell was any indication.

Felicia smiled and shook her head. "You're a guest, yes? You just sit there and keep me company. I usually have my sister-in-law, CoCo, here to talk to me."

"Where are they?"

"CoCo's sister, Alyssa, had her first baby. A boy. She's already e-mailed me pictures of the little angel. Alyssa and her husband, Jackson, live in New Orleans."

"A baby. That's nice." Regret nearly swallowed Monique. She and Kent had wanted a large family but had opted to wait until later. When his business was well-established and he could take time off to spend with the children. Now it was too late.

"Yeah. Luc and CoCo will head back Wednesday, but Tara, CoCo and Alyssa's baby sister, will come back the following week. Tara's married to the sheriff here."

Monique shook her head. "I think I need a diagram to keep up."

Felicia laughed. "It is a bit convoluted, isn't it? I guess I never really thought about it."

A man's chuckle interrupted them. Pastor Bertrand, who had told her that he preferred being called Spence, sat in the living room with Gary, watching some sporting event on television. Their voices blended with the program's, but their bursts of laughter broke out every so often.

"Tell me about yourself." Felicia placed silverware on folded linen napkins.

Wasn't that just a loaded question?

Better to go ahead and get the whole story out—it wasn't as if her past was some big secret. And if she wanted to have a close relationship with her cousin, she needed to trust Felicia. Start at the beginning, that's what her mother always told her. Monique let out a sigh and told Felicia all about Kent, their marriage and his murder. Long after Felicia had set the last plate, she sank into an adjacent chair at the table and stared intently at Monique as she laid out the tale.

"That's terrible. I'm so sorry." Felicia patted Monique's hand. "I can understand some of what you've been through."

"How's that?" Monique fought to keep the tears at bay, having grown extremely tired of crying over the past.

"Before I married Spence, I was engaged to a man. A wonderful man." Emotions laced Felicia's words. "He was murdered."

"How awful." Monique could so relate. "What'd you do?"

"My brother refused to let me wallow in misery." She smiled. "I went ahead and had the surgery that gave me use of my legs so I could get out of the wheelchair I'd spent my life in."

"You were in a wheelchair?"

Again, Felicia's soft smile filled the room. "I have cerebral palsy, diagnosed at birth. Until last year, I'd never walked a step in my life."

Admiration grew in Monique. And respect. "Thank you for sharing this with me. It means a lot."

"You're most welcome. Sometimes it's nice to talk about the painful parts of our past to help us appreciate life and all we have, yes?" Felicia gave Monique's shoulder a squeeze. "But if I don't pull this fricassee off the burner, it'll scorch, and my mother will have a hissy fit."

Monique watched her cousin, her mind replaying Felicia's words. Appreciate life? How? Monique didn't have anything, not even a home anymore. No friends she could depend on. No job to keep her busy during the long days. Not even a pet to keep her company at night. She should really look into getting a cat. Or something. Anything.

"My, something smells marvelous."

Turning, Monique spied an attractive older woman in the doorway. She had to be Felicia's mother—her bone structure was the same. Yet, she had a hardness around the eyes her daughter didn't.

"Hey, Mom. This is Monique Harris, new in town. She moved into the old Pittman house." She nodded at the woman. "Monique, this is my mother, Hattie Trahan."

"Oh, merciful gracious. I heard about the fire. Bless your heart." Hattie tsked.

Monique forced a smile and remained silent.

"What caused it? Faulty wiring? That place was older than Methuselah, and Mr. Pittman never did decent upkeep on it." Hattie moved to work alongside Felicia in bringing dishes to the table.

"No, it wasn't faulty wiring." She really didn't want to have this conversation now. It would lead to the whole reason she'd moved to Lagniappe, and she wasn't ready for that just yet.

"Oh, what was it then?" Hattie turned toward the living room. "Boys, time to wash up."

"Yes, ma'am," came the answering reply.

Hattie faced Monique. "Surely you didn't leave something on the stove or in the oven, did you?"

"No. I hadn't even used the appliances. I'd just moved in earlier in the week."

"Humph. So what caused the fire?" Hattie put her hands on her hips, not moving as she stared at Monique.

"It was arson," Gary said from the doorway.

Felicia and her mother made a collective gasp—in stereo even. For once, Monique appreciated Gary's jumping into the conversation.

"Let's sit down and bless the food first, then maybe Gary or Monique will share the details with us." Spence took his place at the head of the table.

Everyone joined hands while he offered up grace and then everyone loaded their plates in silence, waiting for someone to explain.

Monique took a bite of the delectable chicken fricassee, chewing slowly to buy some time. Red cayenne exploded in her mouth, putting her taste buds on high alert. But the rich flavor of the roux slid down easily. She reached for her sweet iced tea and took a small sip before clearing her throat. "I knew it was arson, even before the report came back."

"How?" asked Felicia.

She tried to figure out how best to get the truth out in the open. *Start at the beginning.*

"Well, I knew it had to be arson because I got a threatening phone call, oh, four days ago. A man who told me to leave."

Felicia and Hattie both sucked in air.

"When I woke up to my house burning, I could smell something odd—out of place—so I knew someone had intentionally set my house on fire. Had followed through on the threat." She swallowed hard and glanced at the deputy. "Gary got confirmation of that yesterday."

She looked at Felicia and Spence. Shock and surprise registered on both their faces, but not a hint of recognition. Nope, they hadn't a clue about her connection to this town. To them. No way could they have set up that call.

"I need to back up a minute, though." She chewed her bottom lip, struggling to pull up a reserve of courage. "I've already told Felicia that I was married and lost my husband in a drive-by shooting. Kent was a private investigator—one of the best."

Felicia leaned forward, ignoring her plate.

"My mother died two years ago, never having told me who my father was. Naturally, with her gone, I wanted a connection. Some sort of family relation." If only they knew how deeply.

"Of course you did, honey." Hattie dropped her fork to her plate, sympathy etched into the creases of her face.

Monique took a deep breath and walked them through her husband tracking down her biological father, obtaining a saliva sample for DNA testing and then Monique visiting him in the Oakdale Federal Prison. She shared with them her pain when he denied being her father, even refusing to undergo a paternity test to prove to him she was his daughter.

"That's awful." Felicia shook her head. "I've been to that prison before and I know how hard it must've been for you."

"I don't think we should talk about this right now, Felicia. This is about Monique." Hattie drained her tea.

"Actually, I'd like to know." Monique stared at Felicia. "Who did you visit in Oakdale?"

"My great-uncle, who murdered my grandfather and my father." Tears wet her eyes, and Spence laid his hand over hers. She sniffled and continued. "And later, I went to see Senator Mouton, the man who killed my fiancé."

"Why would you do that?" Monique blurted out. She couldn't imagine going to see the man who'd killed Kent. Not unless it was to get the truth out of him.

"I needed to forgive him. Really forgive him in my heart." She smiled at her husband. "So I could move into the future with nothing holding me back."

"Oh." Monique dropped her gaze into her lap. Forgive Kent's murderer? Somehow, she didn't think she'd ever reach that point in her life.

"I'm sorry for interrupting, please continue."

Monique stared directly at Felicia. "This is about me, but it's also about you." She included Hattie in her gaze. "And you, as well." Her hands trembled. She clasped them together in her lap.

"What're you talking about?" asked Spence.

"I'd wanted to wait until your brother was here, too, to explain." Monique's eyes implored Felicia.

"Explain what?" Felicia's tone was even.

"My father, the man I visited in Oakdale…" Monique licked her lips. "My father is Justin Trahan."

SEVEN

She certainly knew how to get a crowd's attention. Felicia sat with her mouth gaping. Hattie's eyes were as big as the full salad bowls sitting on the kitchen table. Spence's lips formed a tight line. Silence prevailed.

Monique swallowed hard, wishing she hadn't eaten the spicy meal her cousin had cooked. She glanced at Gary. He, too, sat without speaking, but not a shocked-into-silence quiet. His was more of an understanding-and-waiting-for-the-fallout hush.

All at once, pandemonium erupted in the Bertrand home.

Hattie stood, knocking over her glass. The tea had long since been drunk, but the ice skidded across the table.

"Are you sure?" Spence asked.

"You're not kidding, yes?" Felicia grabbed at errant ice cubes but focused on Monique's face.

"Hang on. Just wait a minute. Let her breathe for a moment." Gary moved to stand next to Monique. She welcomed his warm hand on her shoulder.

"I know it's a shock. Trust me, it was to me, as well, but I assure you it's the truth. I have the DNA test results." She hung her head, her stomach roiling. "Well, I did. They were lost in the fire."

"It's not that we don't believe you, *cher*, it's just quite a surprise is all." Felicia sank into the chair beside her. "I didn't know Justin had fathered any children."

"Well, I declare. It's entirely possible. That *cooyon* chased after women half his age. Girls, really." Hattie fanned herself as she sat again. "Used to drive Beau insane."

"In his defense, I don't think he ever knew about me." Monique struggled to keep her emotions in check. "My mother… well, I think she found out he wasn't exactly interested in becoming a family man, so she never told him."

"Smart woman."

"*Assez,* Mom!" Felicia tossed Hattie a scathing look before shifting her focus back to Monique. "So you surprised Uncle Justin when you went to visit him, yes?"

"Oh, he was surprised all right." Monique shivered at the memory. His face had turned seven shades of red. Eyes had bugged out. He'd talked so fast he'd splattered the Plexiglas with spittle as he all but yelled that she'd better drop her silly notions of being his daughter. Then he'd hung up the phone and shuffled back to the guard. Rejected by a murderer…she really needed to stop letting other people dictate her emotions.

"I apologize. He must've given you a hard time." Felicia's voice soothed. "My great-uncle is many things, but accepting and open aren't on that list."

"Hey, don't apologize. He's *my* father."

And there sat the herd of elephants in the corner.

Silence once again held the room hostage.

Monique waited, counting the long seconds in her head.

Felicia smiled. "No matter how Uncle Justin feels or what he says, you know what this means, yes?"

"W-what?" Monique barely croaked.

"It means you and I are cousins!"

A weight the size of Texas slipped off Monique's shoulders. "I know. That's why I moved to Lagniappe. To meet you and your brother."

Felicia engulfed her in a hug. Not just a glancing hug like telling someone hello, but a real embrace. Monique's heart would explode any minute now.

Spence moved to her other side and hugged her as soon as Felicia let her go. "Welcome to the family."

Yes, indeed, her heart was filled to bursting.

Hattie was next for a hug. "Oh, my, yes, honey. Welcome to the family. This is wonderful news."

"I have a confession to make." How would Felicia react to the truth? Monique didn't have a choice—she had to lay everything out. She'd learned after working with Kent that secrets tore families apart. Even secret thoughts and feelings.

Felicia scrunched her brows. "What?"

"After my house burned, I thought maybe you or your brother might have been involved. Might have made that threatening call." She held her breath, waiting for Felicia to be offended.

"Why would you think such a thing, *cher?*"

"Oh, for mercy's sake, Felicia, think about it." Hattie took her seat and poured herself another glass of tea. "As Justin's daughter, she could file for half the Trahan estate. That would mean less money for you and Luc."

Felicia looked at her mother, then Monique. "You can have anything you want. I would never be involved in such a scam." Hurt flashed in her eyes.

Monique hated that she'd hurt this kind, gentle woman. She laid her hand over Felicia's. "I know that now. But before I met you..."

"Oh."

"I think she was a little in shock, too. Her house had, after all, just been torched," Gary said.

"I don't want any money or anything. I didn't come here for that. I came here to meet y'all, and to get to know you and Luc."

Felicia's smile warmed. "Regardless, when Luc gets back, he'll have the attorney split up the estate to make sure you get your share."

"I don't want it." Couldn't they understand she didn't need it? Didn't want anything that belonged to Just—her father. She just wanted a place to belong, a family. People to love who would love her back.

Spence stood and lifted his plate. "Won't do you any good to argue with her. I know. She always wins."

Felicia laughed and playfully slapped his thigh. "Shush, you. I'm just always right."

He chuckled as he carried dishes to the sink. Gary joined him. Monique moved to help, but Felicia pulled her toward the kitchen door. "The guys can handle cleanup duty. I want to talk to you, get to know you." She glanced at Hattie. "*Allons,* Mom. Let's sit a spell out on the veranda."

Two large wooden rocking chairs bookended the door. A full-size swing hung on one end of the porch. Felicia tugged Monique to the swing. Hattie slipped into the closest rocker.

A breeze drifted across the treated wooden planks. Perfect temperature. Not chilly enough for a coat, but not too warm outside with only a sweater.

"So, what do you do?" Felicia asked once they were settled on the swing.

"Do?"

Hattie chuckled. "She means, as a career."

"Oh." Monique hadn't been ready for that question. "Well, I worked as Kent's assistant in his private investigation business."

"Are you licensed?"

"No. Kent was. I only helped him." Now that she thought about it, she wondered what she wanted to do. So many people pressed her right after his murder to figure out something else to throw herself into. She'd been so focused on seeing his murderer brought to justice, then seeking out her family, that she hadn't considered what she wanted to do for the rest of her life. Thankfully, Kent had had plenty of life insurance. He'd known he had a high-risk profession, and had wanted to be sure she'd be taken care of, no matter what.

"You'll work it out." Felicia smiled, and the day brightened even more. Then she frowned. "Now, tell me about this call."

Monique shrugged, hoping she came across as casual. "He told me to leave. That was it."

"I wonder who would do such a thing. Who knew your number?"

"No one. Well, nobody that I knew of. I'd only gotten the phone service turned on the day before."

"Did you request an unlisted number?"

"I never thought it would be an issue."

Felicia nodded at her bandaged hands. "Do they hurt much?"

"Not really. I think I can stop wrapping my hands in the next day or so." She straightened her legs. "It'll take a few more days for my feet, though."

Hattie cleared her throat and flicked her palms against her slacks. "You are staying, aren't you?"

"Yes. I won't let some freak scare me away." She'd made up her mind—she'd be reactive no more, only proactive. No more being the victim. Now that she knew her family hadn't been involved in the threats against her, that meant it had to be someone from her life before she came to Lagniappe. Running wouldn't get rid of the culprit. It was time to face her fears head-on.

"I'm glad to hear it, but still, it's not safe for a single woman to have a listed number." Felicia wore the most intense expression.

Monique smiled. "I'll get an unlisted number next time." She smoothed the frayed edges of her bandages. "Wow, now I have to start house hunting all over again."

"Are you looking to buy?" Hattie straightened in the rocker.

"Yes. Of course, I'll have to find a place to rent until I can get out and start looking at properties. I can't stay in the motel much longer." She shuddered. "It's not exactly a Sheraton, you know."

Felicia giggled. "*Mais non,* that it's not."

"You shouldn't stay at that motel or in a rental at all," Hattie interjected.

"I have to, Mrs. Trahan. I can't exactly jump into house hunting. I have to meet with my insurance agent about the fire, file claims, talk with the arson investigator and assist in their investigation as much as I can to find out who's responsible, plus meet a Realtor I can work with." The enormity of the tasks ahead nearly suffocated her, but she squared her shoulders and sighed. "All that takes time, and I'm not exactly in top condition to go checking out homes."

"Oh, I understand all that, honey. And please, call me Hattie. I'm saying you should come stay with me until you find a place."

"I couldn't do that." But she was genuinely touched by the offer.

"Nonsense. Since Felicia got married and moved out, I'm all alone in that big rambling place. It's lonely." Hattie tossed her a sad look. "You'd be doing me the favor. I have no one to dote on."

Monique opened her mouth to protest again.

"She's right. There's plenty of room, and honestly, it's part yours because the house was Grandfather's and Uncle Justin's." Felicia nodded with a little too much emphasis.

"I couldn't. I don't want to impose."

Hattie stood in a blur. "No imposition at all. It's settled." She opened the kitchen door. "Spencer, Gary, come on out here. We need your help."

Monique's protests went ignored. What was she supposed to do? If she put her foot down and refused, she'd come across as rude and ungrateful. If she accepted, she'd feel like a burden. A final look at the determination in both Hattie's and Felicia's faces told her resistance would be futile. She'd have to find a place to buy soon.

"Do you really want to go?" Gary took his eyes off the road for a moment to glance at the woman in the passenger seat.

Hattie Trahan had all but ordered him to take Monique back to the motel immediately to gather her things, while she and Felicia went to her house to ready the guest wing.

Monique had been tucked inside his car and they'd been

rushed off so quickly, he hadn't gotten a chance to see if this was what she wanted.

"I know Hattie can be a bit pushy. So if you really don't want to stay with her, now's the time to say something. I can run interference for you if you'd like."

She smiled and his world tilted, in spite of himself. He shouldn't even have gotten this involved. She was a subject. He was a deputy. End of connection.

Except that little things she did kept running through his mind. Like how she tossed that copper hair of hers over her shoulder. Or how she blew her bangs when she was exasperated. Or chewed her bottom lip when she was nervous.

He shouldn't notice these things, much less think about them.

"I think it's nice of her to ask me to stay with her."

Gary laughed. "Ask? If I know Hattie Trahan, and I do, I think the more appropriate word would be *insist*."

She chuckled, as well, the sound of it warm and throaty, sure to haunt his dreams. "Well…seriously, I think it'll be fine. I can ask her about properties for sale, townspeople, all that local stuff."

"Oh, Hattie knows everything. That woman gets the gossip before my mother does."

"Your mother's a very sweet lady."

"Yes, she is." And he couldn't wait to pamper her as she so sorely deserved. He caught Monique smiling at him. "What?"

"Nothing."

"No. What's so amusing?"

"I think it's really nice how close you and your mom are. It's rare to see that type of bond these days."

Heat crept up the back of his neck, and his cheeks burned. He focused on the road. "Well, my mom gave up everything for me. Not many mothers are willing to make so many sacrifices for their kids nowadays."

"That's true." Monique was quiet for a moment, as if caught in the past. "My mom was like that. She raised me on her own, going without so I didn't have to."

"Then you understand."

"I do. You're lucky to still have your mom." Her voice was thick with emotion.

"And I cherish her."

Monique twisted to face him. "You're a good man, Deputy Gary Anderson. I'm glad that I got to meet you. And your mother."

Now heat really scorched his cheeks. "I'm glad I got to meet you, too." He pulled the cruiser into the parking lot of the motel. "If you'll get your stuff together, I'll load it into the back of your vehicle."

"I'd appreciate that. I'll settle up with the front desk and then follow you. I'm assuming you know where Hattie lives?"

They got out of the car, and he looked at her over the hood.

"Everybody knows where everybody lives in Lagniappe, Monique." He loved saying her name. How it felt on his tongue.

"I'm learning that. I mean, Monroe isn't all that big, but you don't know every person in the city."

"City?" He chuckled. "Lagniappe barely qualifies as a town. Most people around these parts call it a community."

"But it's nice." She unlocked the door to her motel room.

"I guess. It's home."

She turned and glanced around, smiling almost to herself. "It *is* home, isn't it?"

EIGHT

Monday mornings were normally the pits all around. But not this one.

Awakening to the sun streaming in past the drapes in the Trahan home—make that mansion—Monique stretched against the smooth, Egyptian cotton sheets. She'd slept soundly, a rare occurrence these days.

Shifting to the side of the bed, she tested her feet. Almost no pain, even when she stood straight and put all her weight down evenly. Nice. She'd left her hands unwrapped last night after her shower. The angry red welts had diminished to pink spots. She fisted and unfisted her hands. No pain at all. Healing, what a wonderful thing.

Tweedle, tweedle, tweedle.

Monique jumped. What in the world?

Tweedle, tweedle, tweedle.

It was coming from her purse on the armoire. Her cell phone. She rushed over and dug it out. "Hello."

"Good morning, it's Gary. How'd you sleep?" The smile in his voice caused butterflies to dance in her stomach.

"Wonderful."

"Good. Listen, I'm meeting with the arson investigator who arrived in town. He has some questions for you, and we wondered if you could meet us out at your property in about thirty minutes?"

"Sure. I'll be there." She closed the phone and headed to the bathroom.

Twenty minutes and a lot of specialty vanilla-scented soap later, Monique bid Hattie goodbye and headed toward her place. No, it wasn't hers. Never had been. To everyone in town it was the old Pittman place. When she bought a new house, she'd make sure there wasn't already a name attached to it. She wanted it to be hers, people knowing she belonged here. She smiled into the sun and tapped her fingernails against the steering wheel.

She pulled into the gravel driveway, her heart clenching. The embers no longer smoldered, yet the air still held the stench of smoke. Gary leaned against the back of his cruiser, talking to another man.

Must be the arson investigator. Monique appraised him as she coasted onto the edge of the grass. He was taller than Gary, who had to be a couple of inches on the upside of six feet, but his shoulders weren't as wide. He shifted to face her as she stepped slowly from the SUV. A full beard and mustache decorated his rugged face. Even from a distance, she could tell that his skin was as coarse as tanned leather.

"Morning. Thanks for meeting us." Gary approached her. While he smiled, the usual warmth was absent. Ah…business mode. She knew it well, having dealt with enough police officers back in Monroe. "This is Bob Costigan, the arson investigator." He nodded at the man. "Mr. Costigan, this is Monique Harris."

She shoved her car keys into her jeans pocket and faced the arson investigator, swallowing back her disappointment at Gary's lack of enthusiasm. "Nice to meet you. How can I help?"

"Let's walk through the site. I need you to tell me what room was where." He picked his way through the rubble, stopping near what was once the living room. Bending, he ran his fingers through the soot, coating the tips, then sniffed his fingers. He straightened. "This is most likely where the fire began. Heavy accelerant was used here."

Was he talking to her, or himself? Maybe he sought confirmation. "When I came into the hall, this part of the house was already in flames."

He glanced over his shoulder at her, then went back to the ruins.

She'd been dismissed. Monique decided right then and there she didn't like Bob Costigan. Not one little bit.

He crept forward and checked the ashes. "No accelerant here."

"That's the hallway."

Nodding, he mumbled, "Interior." He kept moving, turning toward the kitchen, and did his routine once more. "Accelerant present here, as well."

She crossed her arms, tired of following him through the mess. "Exterior wall."

He jerked his attention to her.

"Kitchen."

"I'll get the crew in here, and we'll analyze all the findings." He led the way toward their vehicles, but kept looking back to the rubble. "Accelerant used wasn't graded fuel."

"What does that mean?" Gary asked, finally jumping into the conversation.

"Means it's not regular fuel you can just buy from the gas station." Mr. Costigan reached for a disposable wipe and swiped his hand.

"Then what?" Monique interjected.

The arson investigator pocketed the dirty wipe and stared at her with lowered brows. "I don't know just yet. I'll know once we get some samples to the lab." He reached into his pocket and whipped out a cell phone. Flipping it open, he turned his back to them and took several steps away.

Dismissed again.

"What do you think?" she asked Gary.

"He's the expert. Guess we'll have to wait for test results to come back."

She glanced at the man's back. "I hope he's good."

"I'm sure he is. The fire chief called him in."

"Oh." Continuing to scrutinize him, Monique fingered the sores on her hands. She hoped he would keep digging until the truth came out. She really needed answers.

"Hey, no bandages?" Gary reached for her hands and inspected them. "They look really good."

She trembled at his gentle touch, then pulled her hands free. "They feel much better. And I should be able to stop with the bandages on my feet in another day or so."

"I noticed you weren't hobbling today."

"I think we can go back now." Mr. Costigan had closed and pocketed his phone and approached them. "I've ordered the samples to be taken, talked to the lab about the tests I want run. I need to start my report."

"So what happens now?" Monique wondered about the man's matter-of-fact assessment.

"We wait until the tests come back. Until then, I work on someone's motive to burn down the house."

"Do I need to answer any questions?"

"Not necessary. Deputy Anderson filed his report this morning, and that's all I need for now."

Dismissed yet again. She really disliked this abrupt man.

"Okay, then." She glanced at Gary. "I'll go get some of my stuff done. If you need anything, you have my number."

He opened his mouth as if he wanted to say something, but cut his eyes to the man beside him and clamped his lips together.

Business. All business. She'd dealt with enough cops to know they tried to soften you up with their sweet talk, but then went in for the kill. She should've known he wouldn't be any different, no matter how his clear eyes made her pulse jump.

No, she wouldn't think of him as a man. Just the lawman who handled her case.

Too bad her subconscious wouldn't listen. It kept reminding her of the gentleness in his tone. His subtle laugh lines. How nice he was to his mother.

She slammed the door to her Expedition. Kent was her husband. She'd vowed to love him forever.

But Kent was dead, and she was very much alive.

She glanced at the pile of ash and embers as she started the car.

Alive for now anyway.

"She seemed a bit chummy with you."

Gary snapped up his head to meet Bob Costigan's stare as he leaned against his temporary desk. "What?"

The sheriff's office seemed too small and close with the arson investigator taking up space.

"Ms. Harris. She acted really friendly toward you."

He hadn't seen it, but whatever. "She's new in town and the first week here, her house burns down. I handled the report and saw to it that she found alternate lodging."

"Going out of your way because she's so pretty?"

Heat smeared against the back of his neck. "No, just doing my job."

Bob huffed. "In my experience, when they're really friendly toward you, it's because they're trying to manipulate the investigation."

This guy was a class-A jerk. "Ms. Harris isn't like that. She's had a tough time and moved here to rebuild her life, and what happens? Her house burns down." Although he didn't owe this guy any explanation, he filled Bob in on why Monique had come to Lagniappe, her connections to the area, and how rough she'd had it since arriving.

"Rebuilding her life, huh? She'll need some cash flow for that." Bob scratched his beard. "Doesn't it seem strange to you that she moves in and only days later, she has a house fire that's a total loss of real estate value? On top of that, it's arson. Seems fishy to me."

Indignation on her behalf swelled in Gary's chest. "She received a threatening phone call days before the fire, warning her to leave town."

"So your report says."

"What's that supposed to mean?"

Bob let out a sarcastic chuckle. "There's no proof that call ever happened, is there? The phone had recently been turned on, and there are no phone records for at least twenty-four hours after the activation. There were no witnesses to the call." He shrugged and tossed the case file onto Gary's desk. "Seems mighty convenient to me."

Sure, it looked that way, but Monique wouldn't make up the story. Would she?

"Anyhoo, I've signed the paperwork for you to run her background check and inquiries into her finances. Once you get those back, we'll take it from there."

Gary swallowed hard. "You don't run those yourself?"

"Not in law enforcement. I sign the requests, you order them run." Bob gathered his things and stood. "Don't you know what you're doing?"

Anger stiffened Gary's spine. "I've never had to work with an arson investigator before. Lagniappe doesn't have many fires, and none that were ruled arson that I recall."

Bob huffed. "Well, you pull the background check and financials and give me a copy of those reports. I determine whether to pursue her as an arson suspect or not."

"You really think she could've done this? Burn down her own home? She was inside the house."

"Happens all the time. People need money. Did you notice that SUV she's driving? Newest model. Those things are pricey. People do crazy things. They think if they're inside the house when it catches on fire and they *escape,* then they're no longer a suspect."

Not Monique. She'd come to start her life over. She'd gotten a threatening phone call, warning her to leave town. No, no way.

"I'm going to check and make sure the samples were taken and shipped to the lab. I've requested they identify the accelerant used ASAP. I'll let you know when I get results." He passed his card to Gary. "Call me when you have those reports."

Gary stared after him. Could the man be right?

No, that was just talk.

But Costigan was a seasoned arson investigator. He'd been around this particular block many times. Maybe he could pick up on more than Gary could.

The image of Monique's wide, green eyes with almost invisible eyelashes flashed before him. The pain hidden in the lines of her jaw. The torment etched into the tiny creases around her mouth.

Nope, Monique didn't set her house on fire.

He turned and accessed the sheriff's computer. She'd said she'd been warned, that the fire had been set—which had been confirmed. So far, she'd been nothing but honest and upfront. The old investigator was wrong this time. The sooner he pulled those stupid reports, the sooner Costigan would start looking for the real arsonist.

The one with a grudge of some sort against Monique.

Great. She'd have to wait until the arson investigator completed his business for the insurance company to pay her claim.

Monique shut the phone and stared out the kitchen window, thinking. She hadn't considered that the insurance wouldn't pay out until the arson investigation had closed—she should've known better, but stress had kept her from thinking clearly. What happened if Costigan never found out who set the fire? Would the insurance company keep her wrapped up in red tape and never pay?

"Everything okay, honey?" Hattie poured after-lunch coffee from the sterling silver coffee service.

Monique smiled at her hostess. "It will be. Once we figure out who set my house on fire." She added sugar and cream to her cup.

"Don't you worry about that a'tall. That deputy's a good man. He'll figure it out."

If only Gary were in charge of the investigation. But Bob Costigan seemed to be the one running the show now, and his arrogance had certainly rubbed her the wrong way.

She took a sip of the strong coffee. Really strong. Yet another difference between north and south Louisiana. "I was wondering, Hattie, could you recommend a good real estate agent?"

"Of course, I'd be delighted. But why wouldn't you use the one who sold you the old Pittman place?"

"I used my agent in Monroe. I had no clue who the agent down here even was."

"Well, let's see. There's Amanda Sue Parsons, and Leslie Ann Miliken. Oh, and Barbara Jo Kelly. All of those girls are nice."

And all had double names. Something else that made her feel like she'd moved into a foreign land. "Anybody else?"

"Oh, that nice young man, Parker Fenton."

"Can you get me his number, please? I'd like to get him started in finding me a place."

"Now, honey, you know you don't have to rush outta here. We just found you." Hattie smiled.

"I know. And I really appreciate you letting me stay here." Monique offered a shaky smile. "I really need to get a place of my own, even though I love it here. It's a beautiful home. And the gardens are just gorgeous. I bet they're breathtaking in the summer."

"From spring on, actually. Our designer did a marvelous job with the landscaping. Color-coordinated every flower."

Monique nodded. "I love to work in the yard. That's another reason why I'd really like to get the ball moving on finding my own place. I want to plant some perennials." Hattie's face fell. Better backpedal, double speed. "Of course, seeing how beautiful your yard is, I'll want your opinion and advice."

That got a full smile. "Let me go find his number for you."

Dodged a big one. Monique stood, leaving her coffee on the table, and stared out the window. She'd love to just move on toward the future, start living again. On her terms, not in response to someone else's uninvited influence in her life.

The phone rang, echoing across the hallway. Hattie's heels

tapped on the freshly polished wood floors as she crossed to answer the phone in the parlor just off the dining room. "Hello."

Monique hesitated, hoping this wouldn't be a long call. She'd really like to contact the real estate agent and meet with him later today, if possible.

"Who is this?" The sharp tone of Hattie's voice forced Monique into the hall.

Hattie's free hand hung in a tight fist beside her body. "Who are you?"

"What?" Monique asked as Hattie slammed the phone to its cradle. "Who was that?"

"Prank call." But her hands trembled.

"Hattie, you're upset. Come, sit down." She led the woman to the chaise in the foyer and sat. "Now, who was that?"

"I don't know."

"Man or woman?"

"Man." Hattie shivered.

Monique put her arm around the woman's shoulders. Dread crept up her spine. "What'd he say?"

Hattie shook her head.

"Come on, Hattie, you have to tell me. What did he say?"

"H-he said if I didn't want my house to go up in a puff of smoke, you should leave town."

NINE

Could traffic move any slower?

Gary sighed at the car in front of him that puttered along as if the family were out for a Sunday-afternoon drive. The temptation to turn on his siren hit him strong. He couldn't do that. Monique's call wasn't an emergency. But the fact that the caller had tracked her down and phoned again, threatening Hattie... well, this certainly seemed to indicate Monique wasn't lying about the threatening call from before.

The afternoon sun warmed the crisp January air, lifting the temperature into the sixties at least. Nothing abnormal for the Deep South. Sweat slicked his palms, but it didn't have a thing to do with the mercury level and everything to do with the call he'd taken from Monique.

The old Chevy in front of him finally turned off, and Gary gunned the cruiser's engine, racing toward the Trahan home. He tried to tone down his panic, reminding himself that Monique hadn't sounded stressed when she'd called. Instead, she had sounded calm and collected. He imagined she had to be to keep Hattie in check. The woman certainly had a flair for the dramatic. And the bottle. Monique had said she would call Felicia and Spence to come over, as well.

He made a sharp left down the long driveway, gravel crunching under the tires. The sun's rays flicked shadows amid the large oak trees lining the drive. He parked behind Spence's truck. Monique and Spence met him on the veranda.

"Hattie's pretty shaken up. Felicia's with her." Monique chewed her bottom lip. "I just got here last night. How'd he know I moved out of the motel to here?"

Her eyes were wide, filled with confusion and disbelief. She looked so slight, so frail, as if she could easily break into a million pieces.

Fighting the urge to draw her into his arms and comfort her, Gary pulled out his notebook. "Who did you tell you were coming here?"

"No one but you, Spence and Felicia knew." She licked her lips. "And the desk clerk at the motel. I told her where I'd be because I'd reserved for two weeks and had only stayed for a couple of days. She charged me a fifty-dollar cancellation fee, too."

"Anna Grace." Gary shook his head.

She raised her brows.

"The clerk. Anna Grace." Spence let out a sigh.

"What?" she asked.

Gary opened his notebook and clicked his pen. "Anna Grace's one of the biggest gossips in Vermilion parish. If you told her you were coming to stay here, it was only a matter of minutes after you left before she was on the phone, telling any- and everybody where you'd be." And letting the person who wanted to scare her out of town know exactly where to find her.

"Oh. I didn't know. She asked why I was checking out so early, and I told her that Hattie had offered me a guest room." She let out a sad sigh. "I keep forgetting about the whole gossip thing around these parts."

"Better get used to it. It's a part of life in Lagniappe." Spence reached for the screen door. "Since I'm sure you'll need to talk to Hattie, I'll go see how Felicia's coming along with her." He ducked inside the house.

Alone with Monique, the urge to hold her grew. Gary forced

himself to ignore such emotions. This was business, and he had a case to work. A job to do. A test of his abilities to pass, to prove he hadn't lost his objectivity to a pair of wide green eyes. He began asking the questions—approximately what time had the call come in, what had she heard, what did Hattie tell her the person had said—all facts he'd have to incorporate in his report. And that he'd have to verify later.

"What about the number on caller ID?"

Monique shrugged. "Hattie doesn't subscribe to caller ID."

Not so uncommon in a small town like this. Most people in Lagniappe didn't subscribe, which in police investigations could be a big problem. Like now.

He completed his questions, then led her inside. Hattie sat on the sofa in the sitting room, flanked by Felicia and Spence. Felicia offered Gary a cup of coffee from the pot sitting on the table. He declined—this was no social call.

"Mrs. Trahan." He took the love seat kitty-corner to the sofa. Monique inched down beside him. The gentle wisp of her flowery perfume assailed his senses, and did strange things to his gut.

Clearing his throat and wishing he could free his reactions to her as easily, he tried again. "Mrs. Trahan, I need to ask you a few questions."

"*Oui*. I understand." She took a sip of the coffee Felicia held out for her.

"I'd like you to tell me, in your own words, about the call. Please include an approximate time the call came in, what was said, everything you can recall." He held the pen over his notebook, ready to write as soon as she talked.

"Well, I was heading into the office to get the Realtor's number for Monique. You know, that nice Parker Fenton. Anyway, the phone rang when I was in the hall. I opted to answer the phone in the parlor because it was closer. It was about one-ten or so."

He nodded, not wanting to interrupt and make her lose her momentum.

"When I said hello, at first he didn't say anything. But I could hear someone breathing, so I asked who it was." She shivered. Felicia offered her another sip of coffee while Spence wrapped an afghan around Hattie's shoulders.

She smiled at her son-in-law before returning her attention back to Gary. "I said hello again. And this time he spoke."

Gary waited, knowing not to prompt her and praying none of the people in the room did, either.

"He said, quote, *If you don't want your house to go up in a puff of smoke, Monique should just leave town,* end quote. I asked again who he was, then the line just went dead. He hung up on me."

No mistaking this for a prank call. Or a wrong number.

Gary finished writing and began gathering the details he'd need. "Can you describe his voice?"

"Gravelly, like a smoker's."

He made a note. "What about the volume of his voice?"

"He wasn't whispering, that's for sure, but he wasn't yelling, either. He spoke at a normal level, much like we're talking now."

The grandfather clock chimed two-thirty. Gary turned his head and loosened the muscles in his neck, causing a popping sound.

"What was the tone of his voice? Could you detect any emotion?"

Hattie shuddered. "Ominous. That's the word that comes to mind. He definitely intended to frighten me."

Felicia gripped her mother's hand while Gary jotted down Hattie's impressions. Monique shifted on the love seat, almost distracting him. But he couldn't pay her any mind. Not right now. Even if her close proximity and enticing scent did stupid things to him, like nothing he'd ever experienced.

He tapped his pen against the notebook. "What about pronunciation? Did he talk with a drawl?"

"Well, he spoke with a Cajun accent, if that's what you mean."

That was worth noting. Not many people could imitate the dialect unless they were accustomed to it and spoke it on a regular basis. They couldn't fake it enough for a native not to detect that the inflection was forced.

"Was the connection clear, like from a landline, or was it more distorted like from a cell phone?"

"Landline, if I had to guess. I could hear him very clearly."

A landline would be much easier to track. He drew a star beside this particular note to make sure he pulled the records for the incoming calls to the house. This could be the lead he needed.

"Could you pick up anything from the background? A noise of any sort? Water running, horns, a door chime…anything?"

"You know, there was something in the background."

"What?" He inched to the edge of the love seat. Monique leaned forward, as well.

"Let me think a minute." Hattie closed her eyes, rocking slowly.

Silence ensued save the steady ticking of the grandfather clock in the corner. Monique rested her hand on his shoulder, sending warm jolts down his arm. He refused to let her get to him.

Hattie's eyes popped open. "A match."

"Pardon me?"

"A match being struck, and blown out. That's what I heard in the background."

She had to leave.

Now.

Monique carried the coffee service into the kitchen and set it on the counter with a clank. Tears burned the back of her eyes. She'd brought danger into the home of a sweet lady who'd gone out of her way to be nice.

What had she been thinking, agreeing to stay here? Well, she couldn't any longer. No way would she put Hattie at any more risk.

"Are you okay?" Gary asked from the doorway.

She swiped at the few tears that had managed to escape. "I'm fine." She cleared her throat. "I'm just going to rinse these out."

"This isn't your fault, you know."

Self-pity had been replaced with righteous anger. She spun around to face him. "Yes, it is. That…that jerk wouldn't have bothered Hattie if I had not been here."

"You don't know that."

"Yes, I do. It's the arsonist. And by what Hattie described, it's the same guy who called me."

"I agree. I do think it's the same person."

"And he threatened to burn down this house if *I* don't leave town. Not Hattie. Not Felicia or Spence. *Me.* They were only dragged into this because he's targeting me."

"Which is why I'm not letting you go anywhere."

"How can I stay and put Hattie and her home in danger? I can't do that." She lifted her chin. "I won't."

"I'm going to stay here tonight. Sleep on the sofa."

So what she didn't want to hear. "You shouldn't do that. Then you're putting yourself in danger, too. I can't let you." Why couldn't she just handle things on her own for once?

"I'm a deputy. This is my job."

"Not risking your life when it can be avoided. I can go back to the motel." She bent her head, the tears threatening to consume her. "Or maybe I should leave. Go somewhere else and try to start all over. Again." Running away, letting the creep win—just what she'd vowed she wouldn't allow to happen. But now, putting her new family and friends at risk…it wasn't worth it to take a stand.

"That's nonsense." Felicia pushed past Gary and pulled her into a hug. "You'll stay with me and Spence."

Oh, the hug felt so good. She wanted to cling to her cousin, cry on her shoulder until she was spent. But she couldn't do that. She slipped from Felicia's embrace. "I can't put y'all in danger, either."

"Don't be silly. We've faced worse before and done just fine."

"I can't take that chance, or the responsibility if something did happen." Why couldn't they see that she wanted to protect them? Needed to protect them? Had to do *something* proactive?

Spence joined them in the kitchen, followed by Hattie. "Monique, I don't know about your relationship with Jesus, but there's a certain Scripture that comes to mind. It's Psalms 32, verse 7. *'You are my hiding place; you will protect me from trouble and surround me with songs of deliverance.'* I have to tell you, Felicia and I have been through a lot, separately and together, and God is always there for us."

A sermon she didn't need at the moment. "I appreciate your sharing the Scripture with me, I really do, but that doesn't change the situation right now." She stared into Hattie's face. "You were threatened because of me, and I'm truly sorry."

"That's not your fault, honey," Hattie replied.

Monique gave a sad smile and held up her hand. "Whether or not that's true isn't the issue. If something happened to you— or your house—I'd never forgive myself."

"But you can't go back to the motel. Who'd protect you? At least here, or at our house, you're with family, yes?" Felicia moved closer to her husband, who wound an arm around her shoulders.

Just as Kent had done numerous times.

Her heart screamed at her to absorb the family rallying around her. Yet, her head knew she couldn't. Not without putting every one of them in the line of fire, quite literally.

"I appreciate the offer, I do, but I can't accept it. I have to go." She rushed from the room before they could see the tears, a visible sign of weakness. Running up the stairs, her feet ached for the first time in several hours. She ignored the discomfort until she reached the guest room.

Before she could let her emotions override her common sense, she grabbed her suitcase and shoved clothes and toiletries inside. She was doing the right thing.

When she finished, she barged out of the guest wing and nearly ran smack into Gary. "What're you doing standing here on the landing?"

"Waiting for you." He reached for her suitcase.

"Why?"

He snatched the handle from her and sighed. "Because in case you've forgotten, I *am* the acting sheriff in Lagniappe. This is an open investigation, in which you are the victim. And that makes me responsible for you."

Just as she'd thought—all business.

"Fine, but you can't stop me from leaving."

"I can prohibit you from leaving town. Mr. Costigan hasn't concluded his investigation into the fire yet."

Her sadness gave way to irritation. Perhaps a bit of disappointment? No, she didn't care that he only saw her as a victim, a witness, someone to use to get the information he needed. Well, she shouldn't care.

"I'm not leaving town. I'll go check back into the motel. I'm sure they have a vacancy. Who knows, maybe Anna Grace will refund me the cancellation fee she charged me." She pushed past him to the stairs.

He jerked back as if he'd been slapped. "We'll find out who this guy is. Once we do, I guarantee you, I'll haul him in and see that justice is served for what he's done to you. That's a promise."

His words tugged at her heart. "Look, I'm sorry I snapped at you. It's been a long day, I'm tired and I'm worried about Hattie and Felicia and Spence."

He smiled, righting her world. "It's okay. I understand."

She nodded and descended the stairs. His footfalls echoed behind her.

"But I'm still going to watch over you, whether you like it or not."

TEN

"**Y**ou're making it easy for him to find you."

Monique tossed her suitcase into the backseat of the SUV and spun around to face Gary. Late-afternoon sun bathed them in warmth. "Excuse me?"

"You go back to the motel, and Anna Grace will tell the world." He toed the gravel in the Trahan driveway. "That includes the arsonist, apparently."

True. "Can't I ask her not to say anything?"

He laughed. "Sure, and you can ask the kudzu to quit covering everything, too. Doesn't mean it'll happen."

"Can't you put a gag order on her or something?"

His laughter continued as he shook his head. "Oh, yeah, *that'd* really shut her up. Anna Grace would only tell her best friend…that would be about the entire population of Lagniappe."

"I don't have any other options." She sighed, stress exhausting every fiber of her being. She just wanted to have a normal life—was that too much to ask?

"Let me take you to my mother's."

She stared at him. Hard. Had he lost his mind? "And put her at risk? Are you insane? I don't think so."

"Hear me out. The only way he knew you were with Hattie is because of Anna Grace. Hattie, Felicia and Spence all think you're going to the motel. No one would know you were at my mother's. Especially if you leave now, before he's watching the place and can follow you. I can make sure you don't have a tail on the way to Mom's."

She shook her head. "I can't do that. Not even if there's the slightest chance he'd find out."

"But he wouldn't." He shrugged. "I can crash on the sofa bed for a couple of days, just to make sure you're safe."

A long moment passed before he spoke again. "So, whadda ya say? Will you help put my mind at ease and stay at Mom's, where I can ensure you're safe?"

"I don't think it's a good idea." But he had a point. Going back to the motel could put anyone else staying there at risk once her whereabouts were known, and they wouldn't have the luxury of being forewarned and on alert. At Della's, at least he'd be there to protect his mother. What was the lesser of the evils?

He shot her that charming grin of his. "Come on, say yes. Mom will be thrilled. You'll be safe. I promise."

He sure was making a lot of promises here. Could he keep them? She'd have to trust somebody, because she sure couldn't handle these threats on her own. "Okay. But only if your mother agrees after you tell her the whole story."

"Certainly." He yanked his cell phone from his pocket, flipped it open and pressed a number. "Mom. Hey."

He smiled against the phone. The ache of missing her own mother ripped at Monique's heart. How much she'd give to be able to hear her mother's voice again.

Or Kent's.

"That's fine. Listen, I have a favor to ask." Gary moved to the other side of the cruiser, where Monique couldn't hear his side of the conversation.

Little spurts of discomfort, not quite pain, tingled in her feet. She pushed herself up on the hood of her SUV.

Gary stared at Monique so hard that she wanted to squirm under the intensity.

She turned away and looked out over the bayou. Why

couldn't her life be easy for once? Didn't she deserve normalcy, and maybe, just maybe, happiness?

"She's expecting us." Gary returned to stand in front of her, slipping his phone into his pocket.

"She doesn't mind?" She scooted off the hood, putting more of her weight on her toes.

"Are your feet hurting again?"

"A little." She shrugged. "Not a big deal. I'll be fine once I can clean and rewrap them. So she's okay with me coming?"

"Says she's looking forward to it. Already going to put clean sheets on the bed and lay out some new towels."

"I don't want her to go out of her way. It'll only be for a short while. I'll call that Realtor tomorrow and set up some appointments to look at houses."

"No rush. Mom loves having someone to dote on." He opened his car door. "Just follow me."

Was he out of his ever-loving mind, inviting her to stay at his mom's place?

Gary shook his head as he steered the cruiser toward his mother's house. He checked the rearview mirror—Monique's truck tailed his.

He'd been desperate—that had to be it. Fearful that he couldn't protect her. And he was obligated to protect her because of his job, of course. Not because he was fascinated by her. There, he'd admitted it. He was attracted to her.

Not that he could do a thing about it. She'd made it clear that she wasn't interested. And besides, she wasn't a Christian. That fact alone would have made getting involved with her an impossibility, even if he hadn't still had lingering doubts about her story.

Outside of business, that was.

But in the house he grew up in? Her sleeping in his old bed, in his room? Wasn't that taking his job just a little too far?

She had nowhere else to go. No place she could be safe.

Father God, please guide me. Show me what to do. Help me be Your light in her dark world. Amen.

He turned the car onto his mother's road. Monique stayed right behind him. He hoped he'd done the right thing. What would the sheriff have done in the same circumstances? Would Sheriff Theriot admire him for taking responsibility for the victim, or chide him for taking her home to his momma?

Lifting the radio, he checked in with the dispatcher and found everything quiet at the station. He put in the request to have the phone records for the Trahan home pulled. Missy assured him Mike had everything under control.

Could Mike be a contender for chief deputy?

Mike hadn't been on the payroll long enough…but he did have that past military service on his resume.

Now, more than ever, Gary needed to make sure he handled this case by the book. Even if taking Monique to his mother's appeared to be a conflict of interest.

He couldn't afford to second-guess himself. This would keep her safe until they could get a lead on the arsonist.

Easing on the brakes, he coasted into the driveway, pulling far to the side of the carport. Monique stopped in the middle of the driveway. He parked and got out, motioning for her to park behind his mother's old Honda.

"Here it is, home sweet home." He moved to take her suitcase from her.

"There you are, child." His mother opened the kitchen door and swept Monique in her arms. "I've been worried sick about you. Just get on in the house, now. I've got a nice pot of tea ready."

He smiled to himself. His mother would nurture Monique until she recovered. Of that, he had no doubt. Carrying her suitcase, he followed the ladies inside.

"You just sit right down there on the sofa and let me bring in the tea." Della nodded at him. "Go put her suitcase in the guest room."

"Yes, ma'am." He spared Monique a quick wink before obeying his mother.

He set the suitcase on the dresser, taking in the tidiness of the room. That'd never been the case when it was his, that's for sure. His mother had put an extra blanket at the foot of the bed, and clean towels sat on the sideboard.

"Gary, are you gonna join us for tea or not?"

"Coming." Like he'd risk his mother's wrath? He headed down the hall and back into the living room.

Monique sat on the sofa, her feet propped on a pillow on the coffee table. His mother's doing, of course. Della sat beside her, pouring tea from the little pot he'd gotten her for Christmas two years back. "Come on and sit down, son."

He sat in the chair and accepted the cup from his mother.

She turned back to Monique. "I'm just heartsick over all this nasty business, honey. Are you okay? Really?"

Monique smiled. "I'm fine. I really appreciate you letting me stay here for a few days. I'll call the Realtor tomorrow and start looking for a new place."

"Oh, phooey. Don't you rush into anything. That awful person who set your house on fire is still out there. You shouldn't be alone at a time like this."

"Mom, remember not to tell anyone, not even the ladies in your prayer groups, about Monique being here."

She twisted to glare at him. "Do you think I'm daft?"

"No, ma'am."

Turning back to Monique, she waved him off like a pesky mosquito. "What can I do to help you?"

"Really, letting me stay here is wonderful. I appreciate it so much. I hope it's not too much of an imposition."

"Nonsense. Sometimes this house gets too quiet."

Gary's cell phone chirped. He snapped it off his belt clip and flipped it open. "Anderson."

"It's Mike. You got some faxes that just came through. Look to be about Monique Harris. Thought you might want to know."

"Thanks." He went into the kitchen for some semblance of privacy. "Can you brief me on the content?"

"The NCIC is clean. No history of even so much as a traffic violation. Clean as a whistle."

Relief rolled off him like the dew off the oak trees. "And the financials?"

"Seems like she's got quite a large account."

"Meaning?" Gary leaned against the sink, staring out the window into the backyard.

"For starters, shows that she got almost a million dollars on a life insurance policy some six months ago."

Gary let out a low whistle. "A million bucks? Well, Bob Costigan can strike her name off the suspect list. She doesn't have motive to burn down her own place for the insurance money with that kind of bank balance."

"And she got a cool ninety thousand from the sale of her house in Monroe. The old Pittman place only ran her two-fifty. You do the math. The woman's loaded."

"Thanks, Mike. I'll check in later." He closed the phone and turned to the door.

And met Monique's hostile glare.

"You were checking my bank balances to see if I set fire to my own house?" Anger radiated off her in waves.

"Yes." Gary reminded himself he had nothing to feel guilty about. He was doing his job. "The investigator requested it. This is standard procedure in an arson investigation."

"Did it ever occur to you to ask me? It's no secret. I would've told you."

"This is routine. It's how we do things."

"Yeah, I know all about how the police do things. I've had it up to here with investigations going on behind my back." She jerked her hand toward her throat. "I'd hoped you were different from the rest. What a disappointment to find out you're just like them. Worried about solving cases, no matter what the truth is." She glanced at the doorway.

"Hey, that's unfair."

"Is it? What if you'd discovered I'd been destitute? Flat-out broke? I'd be at the top of the suspect list, wouldn't I? Even though he's called me and Hattie both, I'd still be the main suspect, right?"

"No. I'm working on getting the phone records right now."

"But hey, with my *bank balance,* I could afford to hire some-one to make those calls, right? Isn't that what you guys think? The first suspect is always the right one?"

"That's uncalled for. I'm only doing my job."

"Well, don't let me keep you from it." She spun around and marched down the hall to her room.

His room.

"You really did it this time, didn't you, son?"

He met his mother's harsh stare. She set the tray on the table and shook her head, clucking her tongue.

"Mom, I have a job to do."

"I see that. Boy, I love you dearly, but you sure can be dense sometimes." She gripped the back of a chair. "That girl's hurting and she's scared, although she'll never admit it. She trusted you in her time of need. To find out you went behind her back and pulled some kind of check on her, well, it hurt her feelings."

"I had to do my job."

"Then you could've told her you were going to check into her personal business, that's all I'm saying." She carried the tray to the sink and ran water in the cups. "Ladies don't like men prying in their personal affairs. Makes it seem like you didn't trust her to be honest."

His mouth went dry as he swallowed against the fact that his mother was right.

Once again, he'd tried to do the right thing, and had only managed to mess things up.

ELEVEN

Parker Fenton could turn a lady's head.

Monique tuned out his Realtor's drone, taking in his appearance. His hair flowed like black silk, while his eyes were just as dark. Combined with the sharp contrast of his paler complexion and stark white teeth, she was certain he easily snagged the attention of the opposite sex. Since the package was topped off by his outgoing personality, strong Cajun accent and a physique that bragged of hours spent in a gym, the man could be considered irresistible.

But there was something about him...

"So, we have three houses I think will fit the bill as far as what you're looking for." His smile dazzled her with its brilliance. "Should I go through the preapproval process before we look?"

"Oh. No. That won't be necessary."

His smile slipped for a moment. "Are you sure? I don't mind."

"Just show me the houses. I've already received preapproval."

"Certainly." He nodded and grabbed a notebook filled with computer printouts. Flipping through the pages, he made a ticking noise with his tongue.

A little nervous about buying another house already, she realized he made her even more jumpy. Yet, she had to find a place. She couldn't keep staying with others or at the motel, putting people at risk. Sure, the arsonist would find her when she bought a new house, but at least she wouldn't be endangering anyone else's life. Only hers.

"Ah, here they are." Parker handed the book across the desk to her. "Those three pages have the listings I'm talking about. Look them over and let me know if any of them strike your fancy." He leaned back in his chair, rolling a pencil between his fingers and staring at her in an oh-so-casual way.

She sensed him checking her out. Discomfort seeped into her stomach. He was more interested in her than he should be. She took the listings book and pressed her back into the chair.

The first picture was a lovely log-cabin-type home with a large wraparound porch, but it had too little square footage.

Flipping the page, she studied the second home. It was a nice Colonial, painted a bright yellow, but the home was in a subdivision. She really didn't want neighbors that close.

The third listing looked like a smaller antebellum home, white with two columns on the front. The data sheet noted a nice square footage, no subdivision and the house sat on almost six acres. Monique glanced at the asking price—three hundred thousand. Not bad.

"I'd like to see the third one." She passed the listings book back to Parker.

He raised a brow. "Ah, very nice." His fingers flew over his computer keyboard. "Good, it's vacant, so scheduling a showing shouldn't be difficult."

"How long has it been on the market?"

He punched more keys. "Looks like about six months."

"Does this house have a local history?"

"All houses have histories here, *ma chére*. What exactly do you mean?"

"Well, the house I bought that burned down was always referred to as the old Pittman place. Does this house have a moniker like that?"

"Oh. *Non*. Not that I'm aware of." He typed again on the computer. "The house has been owned by two different owners

over the past two years, so there's likely no family name affili-
ated with the place."

"Good." She crossed her arms over her chest. "How soon
can I see it?" While she appreciated Della's hospitality, she
really needed her own space. Besides, she constantly worried
the arsonist would find her and threaten Della, or worse. She'd
never be able to live with herself if something happened to the
sweet lady who kept trying to wait on her hand and foot.

And if she was going to take a stand, it had to be on her
own two feet.

"If you've got the time, we could head over there now."

She stood. "Let's go."

"You can ride with me." His smile was very attractive, but
something about him made her uneasy.

"I'd prefer to drive myself. Get a feel for the area, ya know?"

"Sure. Follow me." But disappointment laced his expression
as he opened the realty's front door for her. "I'm in the black
Mazda there."

"I'll be right behind you. I'm in the white Expedition."

The drive took only fifteen minutes, most of the time off the
main streets. The bayou, in all her regal glory, lay on the side of
the road. Weeping willows mixed with cypress and oak trees.
Even in the winter, dense vegetation grew as underbrush.
Monique cracked her window despite the chill. The fresh scent
of water and earth drifted past her senses. Surprisingly, the
smells soothed her, filled her with peace.

Parker's car braked before turning onto a gravel driveway
against the bayou. She followed. The driveway curved, and the
house came into view.

It was spectacular. The exterior could use a fresh coat of
paint and the flower beds in front of the porch would need some
serious work, but the house itself was magnificent.

She rolled to a stop behind Parker and got out, taking in the
grapevine-covered gazebo off to the left side of the house. There
appeared to be a little garden bench even farther beyond.

"I know it needs to be cleared a bit, but you can see the potential." Parker headed to the cobblestone walkway to the front porch.

"Yes, I can." She followed him at a much slower pace, relishing the openness and space of the area.

He unlocked the front door with an ornate stained-glass window and allowed her to enter first. "Let me get my bearings, and I'll give you the grand tour."

"Actually, I'd prefer to wander through on my own. If that's okay?"

"Uh, sure. Take your time. I'll just leave my card in the kitchen for the listing Realtor and wait for you down here."

"Thanks." She wandered slowly through the empty house, taking in the vaulted ceilings in the den, the windows facing the bayou on the back side of the house, the hardwood floors that begged for a good polish. The fireplace boasted a marble mantel and hearth. She could already envision curling up beside it and reading a good book on a cold day.

Turning at the end of the hall, Monique found the master suite. And what a suite it was. A built-in armoire filled one entire wall. A large bay window with a bench inside faced the backyard and the bayou. To the right of the entrance was the master bath.

She returned to the hall and took the stairs.

The staircase was cut in a pine of sort, and the handrail was decorated with detailed carvings. On the second floor, there were two more bedrooms, a bathroom and a smaller room that could be used as an office or home gym.

She retreated back down the stairs to check out the kitchen and meet up with Parker, but she already knew. This was home.

"So, what did you think? Any questions?" Parker straightened as she entered the kitchen.

"It's lovely. I'm a little curious why it's been on the market so long when it's a good price."

He shrugged. "It happens sometimes. People move off and don't care. The last family that moved out got relocated with the guy's job. The company bought the house from him and they're firm on the price because that's what they paid for it."

Made sense. "I can see where parts of the house have been updated."

"Actually, according to the listing, there was a major renovation two years ago. Redid the wiring and the plumbing as well as some cosmetic work and landscaping."

She could tell. "Okay. I'd like to put a contract on it."

His eyes all but sparkled. "I'll get back to the office right away and turn the bid in to the seller."

She smiled. "Good. I'll come by this afternoon. How soon do you think we'll hear back?"

"I'll call the listing Realtor myself. I know the appraisal's already been done, as well as the inspection and title search. Everything's waiting on a buyer. We should get an acceptance this afternoon."

"Good." She turned to look around the house one last time before following Parker outside.

Her house.

"Here are the reports you wanted." Gary tossed them onto Bob's temporary desk, anxious to get rid of them. They'd already caused him enough problems.

The arson investigator flipped through them while Gary took a sip of his coffee and settled in behind his desk.

"Well, well, well…the lady has a generous cash flow. Guess she didn't burn her house down to make some moolah."

No, she hadn't. Gary hated that he'd questioned her involvement, even for a second. But that was his job. And if he got chief deputy, he'd have to continue doing such things.

"I got some prelim reports back from the lab."

Gary jerked his attention back to Bob. "And?"

Holding up a piece of paper, the arson investigator read. "Accelerant present is biodiesel."

"Really?"

Bob set the paper on the desk and tented his fingers. "I've done some checking and you have someone locally who makes it."

Gary's pulse spiked. "That narrows the field, yes?"

"I hope so." Bob pushed to his feet. "I'm going to go get a sample from this guy and see if it's a match, then we can go from there."

"Who makes it?"

Bob glanced at a sticky note. "Un-Bio-Believable. Owned by a Terrence Fenton."

"Oh, yeah. I know of him."

"I'll get the sample and send it to the lab, then we'll know if the accelerant used in the fire is from him." He shuffled from the office, making his way down the corridor.

Missy entered the office and handed Gary a printout. "Just came from the phone company."

"Merci." He quickly scanned the information. The call to Hattie's had been made from the pay phone on the main street in town. Anybody could've made that call. Another dead end.

Gary stared at his computer. Who would try to run Monique out of town? His gaze lit on her statements about her husband's death. She seemed convinced the shooter hadn't acted alone. She'd brought up some good points.

Maybe he was looking at the motive of the arsonist all wrong. Maybe, just maybe, he hadn't wanted to scare Monique out of Lagniappe—maybe he only wanted to scare her period, and the threats for her to leave were just an attempt to throw off the investigation. It was possible someone wanted her out of the way period and didn't want to cast suspicion on a connection to her past.

Gary went back to his notes. If Monique had made noise about not believing the shooter acted alone, maybe he *did* have an accomplice, and that accomplice needed her taken out of the equation.

Which meant someone was serious about harming her.

He logged onto the law enforcement database for Monroe, Louisiana, searching for the branch that handled murders. Once he found the number, he lifted the phone and dialed. Then waited.

"Monroe Police Department, how may I direct your call?"

"This is acting sheriff Gary Anderson, from Lagniappe, Louisiana. I'd like to speak to the officer who handled the Kent Harris murder case eleven months ago."

"Hold, please."

Classical music hummed against his ear. He found himself typing the report to the beat of Beethoven.

"This is Investigator Walkin. How may I help you?"

Gary launched into his spiel of who he was and where he was from. "I'd like to ask you a couple of questions regarding the Kent Harris case."

"Yeah, I was in charge of the investigation. Closed case, though."

"I know it's closed, but I had a few questions, if you don't mind?"

"Shoot." The guy's arrogance seeped over the connection.

"I've been reviewing some of the facts and wonder if you ever considered whether the murderer had an accomplice."

"Look, I don't know who you've been talking to, but George Knight confessed to shooting Kent Harris." Indignation blared not only from Walkin's words, but from his tone, as well.

"But doesn't it seem odd that he drove himself and pulled the trigger?"

"Forensics backed up his claim. Gunpowder residue on his right hand. Coroner said the angle of the shot fired jived with what Knight told us in his confession. Open-and-shut case."

"Isn't more than one person normally in the vehicle during a drive-by?"

"What're you trying to say?" Walkin's tone dropped to almost a growl. "Look, we investigated the case by the book. Confession. Murder weapon found. Forensics match. All lined up."

"Sounds very neat and tidy."

"Buddy, I don't know where you're going with this, but I don't have time to talk about what-ifs in a closed case. Knight's in jail. End of story."

"But wh—"

"I've got to go."

The phone slammed in his ear. Gary replaced the handset to its cradle, his mind whirring. Walkin sure sounded defensive about a case he said was open and shut. Having been in law enforcement as long as he had, Gary knew there were always complications, loose ends. But Monique's husband's case sure seemed to have been tied up in a tidy package.

Like Monique, he didn't buy it.

The Louisiana state crime database was his next stop. He typed in the search for Kent Harris, and ordered a copy of the file to be sent to the office. He'd read the case file himself and see what inconsistencies he could find.

Mike stuck his head in the door. "Hey, wanna grab lunch? It's quiet around here and I'm starving."

Gary glanced at the clock. "It's only eleven."

"I'm starving." Mike sucked in his cheeks, looking like a fish. "I'm gonna waste away if I don't eat."

Chuckling, Gary stood. "Why not?"

After notifying the dispatcher they were taking lunch, they walked across the street to the little diner. A bell tinkled as they opened the door, and the smell of grease and pepper slammed against them. A waitress motioned them to a corner table with a curt nod while she delivered drinks to a neighboring table.

"Now I'm really hungry."

Gary laughed at the man who might be his competition. But it was hard not to like Mike. Built like a middle linebacker, the ex-military man was funny and outgoing.

The waitress dropped two menus on the table, told them the special of the day was meat loaf, and took their drink orders before scuttling off to the kitchen. She returned with their soft drinks.

"I'm having the jumbo burger with japs and fries. Wait, the onion rings." Mike closed the menu. "I'm gonna have both."

Gary shook his head. "I'll have an open-faced Reuben and salad." Unlike his colleague, his physique couldn't process so much grease and fat. He glanced over the restaurant, nodding at those he made eye contact with.

Then he froze.

Monique sat in a booth on the opposite side of the room. She had her face scrunched in concentration as she stared at her date.

Her date was a very handsome man, who looked at her as if he wanted to gobble her up for lunch.

Gary lost his appetite, and the greasy smell turned his stomach.

Who was that guy? Gary recognized him from around town, but didn't know who he was. Better yet, why was Monique with him and staring at him with such rapt attention?

TWELVE

Parker's phone buzzed.

"Hello, Parker Fenton here." He smiled and nodded at Monique. His leering unnerved her, but she pasted a smile on her face.

"Yes, and the buyer would like to close as soon as possible." Another pause. "Hold on a moment and I'll ask."

He pressed a button and grinned. "The seller will close as soon as your lender has processed all the paperwork and everything's good to go. Who's the lender, so I can give you an estimate of how quickly they'll work?"

"I can have a cashier's check for them this afternoon. Is that soon enough?" Monique sat back. The reaction would be immediate.

He didn't disappoint. His mouth dropped before he checked himself and pressed a button. "We can have the cashier's check ready this afternoon. Get back with your seller and see if that will work for them. Fax me the closing paperwork at the office. Thanks." He shut the phone. "You don't need funding, do you?"

"No."

"Why didn't you tell me?"

"Because you didn't need to know. I told you I had preapproval. I just didn't tell you I actually had the money in hand." She took a sip of her iced tea, which was nearly gone. Only the melting ice provided any liquid.

A frown marred his handsome features. "I see."

No, he didn't, but she didn't feel obligated to explain. It was none of his business, not that she tried to be mean or rude. She just wanted to conduct her business and be done.

She let her gaze dance over the other occupants of the diner. Her eyes collided with Gary's.

Now she wished she hadn't eaten that entire salad—something seemed to be caught in her throat.

Gary stared at her, openly and unabashedly. She wanted to squirm in her seat, but thought better of it. She'd been hard on him yesterday. After tossing and turning most of the night, she realized he'd only been doing his job. At least he checked into every suspect, which was more than she could say about the police back in Monroe.

Pushing down her unease, she smiled and waved Gary over.

He said something to the other man decked out in the deputy uniform before walking over. "Surprised to see you here."

She motioned him to the vacant chair beside her. "Deputy Gary Anderson, you know Parker Fenton?"

"Not officially." Gary offered his hand. Parker stared at it a moment before shaking.

"Parker showed me a house today. One I've put a contract on."

"Oh?" Gary turned his head to peer at the other man.

While Parker did his song and dance about the property, Monique sensed the competitive tension between the men. They were close in age, both handsome in their own way, both physically fit. Either would be a good catch for a woman.

But something about Parker didn't seem as appealing to her. Especially when placed side by side next to Gary. He just didn't measure up.

"Where, exactly, is the house?" Gary asked.

Parker jumped in before she could describe the place. "Out off Harden."

"Oh, yeah. I know the area. Really nice places out that way." He scrutinized her, making her itch to fidget again. He had a certain look that held a question, but one he wouldn't ask. "So you liked the place that much?"

She smiled at Gary. "It feels like home."

His returning smile warmed her heart. "What attorney are you going to use to do the closing?"

Huh? "Attorney? What about a title company?" Confusion washed over her.

Parker cleared his throat. "Well, we can use a title company if you'd like, but you won't be able to close today. We don't have one locally. I can request a rep from one in another city to come over."

"But that'd take extra days, right?"

"Yes."

"Is Mom driving you up the wall already?" Gary asked.

She put her hand on his arm. "No, nothing like that. I just need my space. I've lived alone for several months now, and have gotten quite used to it." Could he think she didn't like his mother, or wasn't appreciative of being allowed to stay with her? "Your mom's great, and I really appreciate her hospitality, but…"

"Hey, I totally understand. I'd go nuts if I had a roommate."

"Wait a minute—you're staying with *his* mother?" Parker's eyes were wide, and a crease etched deep between his brows.

She didn't owe him any explanation. "Long story, but yes." She placed her crumpled napkin in her empty bowl. "So, I can use an attorney for the closing?"

"Most around these parts could handle it. I can recommend several I've worked with."

"Try Dwayne Williams," Gary interrupted.

"You know him?" Monique asked.

"He handled some issues for CoCo LeBlanc *Trahan* a couple of years ago." His wink almost went undetected.

But she'd caught the gesture and knew what he was getting at.

Parker cleared his throat. "I've never worked with him before. We normally use Mr. Canatara. He's a good man and very well up—"

"I'll call Mr. Williams's office as soon as I leave here." She winked back at Gary.

"Good." He glanced over his shoulder, then stood. "Well, looks like my lunch is arriving, so I'd better go." He nodded at Parker. "Nice meeting you."

His eyes softened as he smiled at her. "I'll talk to you later."

She couldn't stop herself from watching him saunter across the crowded diner. Something about the way her heart hiccupped when he smiled and winked at her made her believe there could be life, and romance, after Kent.

Feeling this spark after only knowing him five days? She must be more stressed than she'd thought.

When it rained, it poured.

Gary sifted through the paperwork mounting on his desk. He and Mike had only been gone an hour, yet his in-box nearly overflowed. Little things but ones that demanded an answer.

Just as he neared the bottom of the stack, Bob Costigan strolled into the office. "Got the sample to the lab. They should be able to let me know in the morning if it matches the accelerant used in the Harris fire."

"Good." He signed the last piece of paper and shoved it in the out-box for Missy to pick up later. "So where does this leave us in the investigation?"

"For now, we have to assume Ms. Harris isn't involved in the arson."

"I don't believe she is."

"Really?" Bob shook his head and slumped into the chair opposite his temporary desk. "Either way, a lot hinges on the sample being a match. I went ahead and requested a list of buyers of the diesel from Mr. Fenton."

The name… "Wait a minute. Terrence Fenton. I think I met his son today."

"Isn't that a coincidence?"

Gary didn't believe in coincidences—he believed everything that happened was part of God's master plan.

So what did it mean that both Fenton men could be linked to Monique? His law enforcement curiosity kicked in.

"We should order a background check on Terrence Fenton, just in case."

Bob finally cracked a grin. "You beat me to the punch. I was going to ask you to pull the report."

Amazing, the man's face didn't split. Gary reached for the request form.

"Of course, if the sample isn't a match, that report means nothing."

"But if it is, we're a step ahead of the game."

"Yep, and every day counts. We're already behind by four days, but that's always the way it is in my line of work." Bob leaned the wooden chair back on two legs.

"Don't remind me."

"Does the son work with the father?"

"Nope. He's a real estate agent."

"Father makes fuel, son sells houses. Odd combo, wouldn't you say?"

Gary was saved from answering by his cell phone. "Anderson."

"Well, hello there, Deputy."

Heat spread across his neck at the sound of Monique's voice. He only prayed it didn't reach his cheeks in front of Bob. "Hi, yourself."

"I wondered if you'd like to run out to the house I'm now the proud owner of, as of four-thirty today."

"So the closing happened?"

"I called Mr. Williams. Thank you for recommending him. He's really nice and knew his stuff."

"I know CoCo was very pleased with the work he did for her. Coming from her, that's a high compliment."

"You're making me nervous to meet her."

Would he ever learn to think before he spoke? "No, you'll love her and she'll adore you. I meant her recommendations are genuine."

"Well, Mr. Williams was exactly what I needed, so thanks."

"No problem. I didn't want you to use someone that Realtor uses all the time. No telling what kind of behind-the-scenes kickbacks are going on."

"Do you have a report on Parker? I didn't know when I called him. I ju—"

"Oh, nothing like that. He just gave off a strange vibe." Yeah, commonly referred to as the green-eyed monster, but Gary wasn't ready to address his feelings and why Parker stirred up jealousy. Not now. Not until he'd caught Monique's arsonist.

"I noticed that a bit, too." She let out a low sigh. "So, would you like to come see my house? I'd really like to get your opinion."

Something unfamiliar curled inside him. She wanted *his* opinion? "Sure." He glanced at his empty in-box. "I'm finishing up here. I can meet you there in fifteen minutes."

"You know where it is?"

"Off Harden, from what Fenton said."

"Right on Wyatt Lane. I'll see you shortly. Bye." The smile in her voice came through the connection.

And filled him with trepidation. Off Harden, right on Wyatt Lane? That would mean… No, it couldn't be. Especially after just having thoughts about coincidences. It had to be a different house.

"Got a hot date?" Bob's voice jarred him back to reality.

"No." But the heat moved up his neck to the back of his head. "Only helping a friend out who needs a second opinion on buying a house."

"Couldn't help but overhear the name Fenton. Ought to see what you can find out about him while you're there."

He stood and straightened the papers in the out-box. "I don't think he'll be there."

Bob snorted.

"Well, if he's there, I'll see what I can find out."

Bob rose out of the chair. "I'm going back to the fire site. Sometimes when I'm alone, I can detect more."

Gary hesitated. Monique or his job? "Would you like me to go with you?"

"I said, when I'm alone I can detect more."

"Oh. Okay, then. See you tomorrow." He didn't wait for a reply, just headed down the hall, checked out with Missy to let her know all the paperwork had been completed and crossed the parking lot.

The late-afternoon sun teased the tree branches as he drove out of town. He'd always appreciated how beautiful this area was. The bayou backing up to the land meant no neighbors would move in behind. As he thought of Monique, it occurred to him that the location, while quiet and breathtaking, also left the homes isolated. Someone could creep in undetected.

And there was still the possibility the house… No, it *had* to be a different house.

The sense of foreboding stayed with him as he turned onto Wyatt Lane. He slowed, admiring the stately homes. Farther down, the houses became smaller. Almost at the dead end, he spied Monique's white SUV parked at the end of a driveway.

She stuck her hand out the window, waving. Oh, no. It *was* the house.

He turned in and followed her slow pace, taking in the lay of the land. While the property hadn't exactly been totally re-landscaped, it didn't look like it had when the original owner had lived here.

Monique bounced out of her vehicle and met him, a huge smile plastered across her face. How could he tell her?

"Isn't it wonderful?" She grabbed his hand and tugged him around the side of the house. "Look at this—a gazebo and a flower garden. With a bench and everything." Excitement made her cheeks flush.

He planted his feet as he stared at the bayou butting up against the land in the backyard. The palms lining the water's edge had grown quite a bit since the last time he'd been there, making the bayou appear more ominous.

"Come on, you have to see the inside. It's amazing." She pulled him back to the front yard. "Now, I'll want to get the porch totally refinished and treated. And the flower beds will need a lot of attention, but I think Hattie will take the task in hand and give me some great direction."

"Um, Monique…about this house. Y—"

"Don't say anything until you see it." She jammed a key into the front door and turned the lock. "At least we still have some daylight. I'll have the electricity turned on in the morning." She stood in the living room. "It's really small. I'm not sure why, because the rest of the house is spacious and airy. But I'll use this as a sitting room."

She glowed like a kid on Christmas morning. "You have to see the master bedroom. It's amazing." She led the way down the hall.

Dread slowed his steps. Did she get a title search? Did she know who had owned it before? Surely she wouldn't have bought the house if she'd known.

"Look at this bay window." She crossed her arms, hugging herself. "I want to get one of those big wooden rockers to put right here, so I can look out over the bayou whenever I want. It's so peaceful."

"Monique."

She spun and faced him, wearing a frown. "What's wrong? Don't you like the house?"

"I like the house."

"Then what?"

He felt like bayou scum. "It's getting dark in here. Let's go back outside."

"Okay." She followed him in silence.

Gary hated to spoil this for her, would do anything not to have to say anything, but he didn't have a choice. She had a right to know. She needed to know.

Once out on the porch, she planted her feet. "You're scaring me. What's wrong?"

"This house. Do you know who the original owner was?"

"No." She sucked in air. "Who?"

"Justin Trahan, your father."

THIRTEEN

The world tilted backward on its axis, and she swayed.

This couldn't be happening.

Gary grabbed and steadied her in his strong arms. "Are you okay?"

"A-are you sure this was his house?"

"Positive. He tried to kill Luc in the backyard near the bayou."

Oh, just great. She was going to be sick any minute now.

"I'm sorry. I shouldn't have just blurted that out." He tightened his embrace, pulling her closer to him.

She could hear—no, feel—his heartbeat. The clean scent of aftershave and deodorant wrapped around her as tangible as his arms. She relaxed, drawing on his strength.

He smoothed her hair and slowly rocked with her back and forth.

Laying her head against his chest, she sighed, letting go of her concerns. Her worries. Her fears.

His lips grazed the top of her head.

She jerked out of his hold. What had she been thinking? Allowing herself to get too comfortable. Too dependent on his security. She had to handle things on her own. She ran a hand over her hair. "I can't believe I bought his house. He wasn't listed as the seller."

"No, he wouldn't be." He wrapped an arm around her shoulders and led her toward the vehicles. "Luc and Felicia sold his house to a young family as soon as he was convicted and imprisoned. Everything he owned returned to the Trahan estate, which as the only legal heirs, they manage." He leaned against the hood of the vehicle. "Well, I imagine you're an heir now, too."

"How ironic, huh? That I bought his house when, had I known he was my father a couple of years ago, I could have inherited it."

"Yeah."

"What am I going to do?" Dismay shrouded her heart like the overgrown grapevines covering the gazebo. "I can't live here."

"Why not?"

Was he crazy? Hadn't he just told her about her father trying to kill Luc in the backyard? "I don't know. It's creepy."

"You told me today it felt like home."

She shuddered. Had this been yet another sign she'd missed? "But now, knowing the truth…"

"The house doesn't look like it did when Justin lived here. The two families that lived here since did a lot of renovating."

"That's what Parker said." But still…

"And you could do what you want with the place. Make it really yours. Put your mark on it."

"What will Felicia and Luc think, though?" She cared what her family thought. Even if she'd just met them.

"That you bought a house you liked."

"Even though Luc was almost killed here?"

"He knows you had nothing to do with that."

"But it might still bother him. Be a reminder and all that." And she'd hoped to connect with Luc and his wife as she had with Felicia and Spence. She'd had visions of cookouts in the backyard, visiting around the flower gardens—what would Hattie think?

"I know them. If anything, they'll both be upset you actually had to pay for the property."

She glanced at the house. She did love it. Had felt a kinship to it as soon as she'd laid eyes on it. Now she knew why. Was this God's ironic joke on her?

Gary took hold of her hands. "Look, the decision is yours, but you've paid good money for this house. I think you should talk to Felicia if it'll make you feel better. Get her reaction. Then, if you feel okay about staying, go ahead and move in. See if it works for you."

Did he have to be so logical as well as handsome? And considerate? And strong? She tucked her hands in her pockets.

"I'm sorry. Did I hurt your sores?"

What? "Oh. No. They're practically healed. And my feet are almost as good."

"Just wanted to make sure." He tucked his thumbs into his belt loops. "I have a feeling it's all gonna be fine, but I thought you would want to know."

"Oh, most definitely. I'll call Felicia tonight. I can't believe… of all the houses, I had to p—"

"Well, in case you haven't noticed, Lagniappe isn't exactly a hoppin' real estate market."

"Parker only had three houses to show me."

"And you picked this one. Call Felicia. I guarantee she'll be okay with this."

Maybe he was right. It could even be that she needed to be in this house. Put the past to rest. *Really* start over, once and for all. "I'll do that." She glanced up at him from beneath her eyelashes. "Thanks for telling me. And for before. I got rather dizzy."

"No problem."

An odd silence covered the space between them. But she couldn't admit that him holding her had felt good. Too good.

"Hey, I called the Monroe Police Department today."

That grabbed her attention. "Did you now?" Interesting.

"Talked to Investigator Walkin."

"What were you being punished for?"

He chuckled. "I wanted to know more about your husband's murder."

She hesitated. "Why?"

"Because what you told me about the case didn't make sense."

"What part?"

"Everything came together rather quickly with all the loose ends tied up."

Relief flooded her. "So you think I'm onto something?"

He held up a finger. "I'm only checking all possible scenarios."

No promises. That wasn't a surprise. "What'd you think of Walkin?"

"Honestly? He came across as very arrogant and defensive."

"That's pretty much the way he is in person, too. Did you find out anything useful?"

"There are a lot of things that are too neat." He stared out over the bayou. "I requested the case file."

"Really?" So she'd been right—it did seem fishy. Finally, someone who understood.

"I wanted you to know. In case you heard about it. I wanted you to know why I ordered it."

Guilt washed over her. "I'm sorry for chewing you out about my background check. I know you were only doing your job."

"Let's forget about it."

She smiled, his easy manner making her want him to hold her again.

No, she shouldn't even think this way. Here they were, discussing Kent's murder, and the next minute she thought about being in his arms? What kind of woman was she?

A very confused one.

His cell phone rang. "Anderson."

She stared back at the house again. Despite what she knew, she really did love it.

"She's here with me. We're on our way." He snapped the phone shut and slipped it back into his belt clip. "That was Mom, worried about you. And she didn't want you to think she was checking up on you, so didn't call your cell."

"I should've told her I'd be late. I'm such a horrible house-guest."

"No. You just aren't used to being a houseguest. She has supper ready." He nudged her shoulder with his. "Come on, she made étouffée. And she's a mean cook."

Her stomach rumbled. Appalled, she covered her mouth with her hand. Gary burst out laughing.

"Let's go. Obviously, you're as hungry as I am."

"I'll follow you." She slipped into her SUV and turned around, waited for him to do the same, then followed him down the gravel driveway. She caught sight of her house in the rearview mirror.

If Felicia didn't have a problem with her staying in the house, she'd start ordering furniture tomorrow. She'd do as Gary suggested—make it hers.

Despite its original owner.

Was he overstepping his bounds?

On the drive home, he'd called his mother and asked if he could invite two more for supper. Of course, she'd been enthusiastic about more guests. Then he'd called Felicia and Spence and asked them. They'd been more than happy to agree.

Now, turning onto the road to his mother's house, little shards of doubt nudged against his mind. Maybe he should have waited and asked Monique what she wanted. He'd just seen her total excitement, then her abject disappointment. He *knew* Felicia would encourage her to keep the house and make her feel comfortable with that decision, and he wanted to ease her mind as soon as possible.

But would she be upset over his meddling in her personal business? Again?

He pulled into his mother's driveway and parked. He'd better warn Monique about what he'd done, or she might really blow up at him—and he'd deserve it.

She still wore the uncertain expression she'd had back at the house, the complete opposite of the exhilaration she'd had before he'd crushed her with the news. Yeah, he'd made the right decision in inviting Felicia over to reassure her, even if Monique didn't see it that way yet.

"Before we go in, I need to tell you something."

Hesitation coated her like moss on the cypress trees. "I don't know if I'm up for more revelations right now."

Uh-oh. Again he doubted his actions. No, his heart had been in the right place. "I know you're very uncertain, unsure what to do."

"Yeah, I am."

"I know you said you'd call Felicia tonight and talk to her about it."

"I think that's really the best thing, don't you? She and Luc would be the ones who could be most hurt by memories surrounding the house."

"I do think it's a good idea, which is why I called and invited her and Spence over for supper." He waited for the explosion.

"Tonight?" Her amazing green eyes grew wider than lily pads. Darkness crept into the edges of the irises.

He'd better start explaining. Quick. "I think the conversation will go better in person. So you can read her body language, yes? Since you've just met, you might not be able to pick up subtleties over the phone that you can in person."

She leaned against the side of her truck, remaining silent. Seconds fell off the clock. Minutes. Finally, she let out a heavy sigh. "I want to be angry with you for interfering, I really do, but it's hard when you use logic on me."

He held his breath.

"I'm irritated you act without checking with me first, but you're right, the conversation really should take place in person."

At least she wasn't going to erupt. Good thing, because Spence's SUV whipped into the driveway moments later. Felicia burst from the car and hugged Monique. "I'm so tickled Gary called. I've been thinking about you all day, *cher.* How're you?"

Monique smiled, the cloud of insecurity lifting from her expression. "I have so much to tell you, but let's go in and eat. Della must be wondering what's keeping us."

Gary let the ladies enter first, then Spence. His steps quickened as the enticing aroma of his mother's special étouffée teased his senses, making his taste buds tingle in anticipation.

After everyone washed up and took a seat at the table, his mother asked Spence to offer grace. He took Monique's hand, noticing the slight tremor against his palm as Spence gave praises to God.

Soon, bowls were filled to overflowing and the compliments flew to Della. In her element, his mother patted her hair and beamed.

Monique took a big spoonful, chewed, then turned red in the face. Her eyes watered. She swallowed. Coughing followed.

Spence, sitting beside her, slapped her back. "Go down the wrong pipe?"

She shook her head, reaching for the glass of iced tea. She gulped it down without taking a breath before blowing slowly. "Wow, that's spicy."

A collective laugh rose from the table. Della shook her head. "Oh, honey, this is the mild recipe."

"Mild?" Her voice squeaked.

Felicia patted her hand. "Don't worry, we'll turn you into a pepper-belly real quick, yes?" She reached for her own tea. "So, tell me what's going on."

"Well…" Monique dabbed her mouth and the corners of her eyes with her napkin. She looked around the table, ending her focus on her cousin. "I bought a house today."

Everyone spoke at once—

"Awesome. Where?"

"When can we see it?"

"You didn't have to rush into anything. You can stay here for as long as you like."

Gary shook his head. This was becoming quite common around Monique.

She giggled. "Hang on, I'll tell you everything." The darkness returned to her eyes, which sought him out.

He winked, clenching his fist to squelch the urge to reach across the table and hold her hand. But she had to do this by herself.

Her words tumbled over each other as she told them everything—falling in love with a house on sight, buying it in one day, taking Gary to see the house and then learning it'd been Justin's. When she finished, she was out of breath.

Silence prevailed but for only a short moment.

Felicia's eyes filled with moisture. "This is perfect. A new way to build positive memories, yes? But as soon as Luc gets home tomorrow, we'll contact the estate attorney. You should not pay for what should be yours to begin with. The trust will reimburse you for the selling price."

He'd been right. The relief marched across Monique's face.

Gary wasn't able to explain why his heart thrummed over her being reassured. Well, he probably could, but wouldn't. Not yet.

FOURTEEN

"It's a match."

Gary looked up from his computer and stared at Bob Costigan, standing in the sheriff's office doorway. "Huh?"

Bob shot him a look of disgust. "The samples from Fenton's place? It's a match to the accelerant used in the Harris fire."

"Then we need to talk to Mr. Fenton. Get information on who he's selling to."

"Why do you think I'm here? Fenton stonewalled me—said he didn't have to give me information. Maybe your badge will change his mind. Get off your duff, and let's go."

"Hang on, let me see if his background check has come back yet." He lifted the phone and buzzed the intercom. "Missy, have you gotten the report on Fenton yet?"

The sound of shuffling papers drowned out her humming. "Yep, came in this morning with the FedEx deliveries."

He wanted to sigh. She should've sent that report to his office as soon as it came in. "I'll come get it." He dropped the phone back to its cradle and nodded at Bob. "Just a second. We got the report in."

Making fast tracks down the hall to the front reception area, Gary took the folder from Missy's outstretched hand. He flipped through pages as he walked back to the office. No outstandings. No priors, unless you counted the DUI eight years ago.

"Anything?" Bob asked as Gary returned to the office.

"Nothing useful." He passed the folder to Bob, who perused it.

"Worthless. Let's go talk to him."

Gary logged off his system, told Mike where he would be and followed Bob out the door. "Let's take the cruiser, looks more official."

Bob nodded and headed to the car. "I hope he's more cooperative with you along."

"I'd hate to have to hunt down a judge to get a warrant to look over his client list."

Bob only grunted as Gary spun the cruiser toward Un-Bio-Believable. "I still think there's an angle between father, son and Ms. Harris."

Discord filled Gary's senses. He'd tried to disregard Parker because of that uncommon feeling of jealousy, but what if his cop's instinct caused his dislike of the guy? What were the odds that Monique's Realtor was the son of the man who sold the accelerant used to burn down her first house in Lagniappe? He kept reminding himself that she'd been the one to contact Parker, based on Hattie's recommendation, not the other way around. Still…

"I guess we'll find out more when we talk to Terrence Fenton." Gary pushed down his personal feelings and turned onto the dead-end road on the edge of town Bob had indicated.

"Well, here we are." The arson investigator pointed at a corner lot just ahead. "That's the place."

A big warehouse stood alone on the property, with two large holding tanks, approximately six feet tall and eight feet in diameter. Together, they probably held about a thousand gallons of the fuel.

Gary whipped the car into the lot, then he and Bob headed into the office. The room reeked, like walking into a bring-a-burger joint and sidling up to the deep fryers.

A freestanding counter divided the small space. Two metal folding chairs leaned against the wall by the door with a single window sporting dirty panes, while a desk and a small computer setup stood on the other side. A lone, ancient copier occupied the corner.

A man with thinning gray hair and skin the texture of leather sat behind the desk. He glanced up, recognized Bob and stood. Apprehension jumped in his body language. "Can I help you?"

"We've matched your biodiesel fuel to that used as an accelerant in an arson," Bob said.

Although in uniform, Gary flashed his badge for good measure. "We'd like to look over your client list. You do keep track of who you sell the fuel to, yes?"

"I keep records. Have to, for tax purposes." The balding man with eyes entirely too close together hedged. "But my clients like their privacy."

Gary let out a sigh. If fewer people watched crime-type television shows, his job would be so much easier. He glanced around the small-time operation, wondering if Fenton kept up to date with all the OSHA regulations. Time to find out. "I guess I can go get a warrant. I just wanted to avoid bringing legal attention to your business."

Terrence's beady eyes narrowed. "What do you mean, legal attention?"

"Oh, we have a mountain of paperwork we have to go through to get a warrant. Every time we fill out everything, the system feels like it needs to check up on all aspects of the company we put in the paperwork. OSHA, IRS...you know, all the alphabet-soupers." He shrugged as if he didn't care one way or the other. "I thought maybe you'd like to avoid all that hassle, but it doesn't matter to me."

Terrence's cheeks inflated like a puffer fish. "You know, I don't see an issue with letting you have a peek at my sales records over the past few weeks."

Bingo! Gary smiled. "We'd sure appreciate that."

The business owner set a large, blue ledger on the counter and flipped it open. He stopped on a page. "These are my buyers for the past month." He turned the book toward Gary and Bob.

Gary took out his notebook and copied down names.

"Shows eight buyers," Bob commented.

"Yep, that sounds about right."

"All of these regulars of yours?" Gary asked.

"Ummm." Terrence pulled a pair of wire-rimmed glasses from his pocket and perched them on the end of his nose. "That one, and him, oh, and them, too, are."

Gary made checks in his notes beside the names Terrence had indicated.

Bob studied the ledger. "So, only two of these are new customers?" He leaned closer to the paper and read. "Kevin Haynie and Niles Patterson. That right?"

"Yep, them two I didn't know."

Gary peered at his notes. "Do the buyers have to fill out any paperwork on purchases?"

"Order forms, yeah."

"May we have a copy of the order forms on Haynie and Patterson?"

Terrence hedged again. "Giving you a copy, with their addresses and all…that's more than letting you have a peek."

"Suit yourself. Warrant or no, it's your call." Gary held his breath, hoping the old man bought the bluff. A warrant would take a bit and Gary could feel the adrenaline spurting through his veins—they were on the right track, he felt it.

Terrence scratched hair that had long since fallen out. "I guess just those two orders won't be a problem. After all, it's not like they're regulars or anything."

Gary waited while the man found the invoices, made copies on the battered copier, then handed them over.

"We certainly appreciate your help." Gary handed his business card to Terrence. "If you think of anything else, anybody maybe not listed on your ledger who bought some fuel the past month or so, please give me a call."

Terrence pocketed the card. Gary could almost envision him ripping it up and throwing it away as soon as they were out the door. He couldn't do anything about that. Nodding to Bob, he turned and left the musky building.

Bob wandered toward the tanks instead of the cruiser.

"What're you doing?"

"Checking out the system." Bob leaned over and inspected the pump on top.

"And?" Gary shifted his weight and glanced toward the building. Was Terrence standing at that single window, staring at them and wondering what they were doing scrutinizing his setup without a warrant?

"Well, I don't think someone could just walk up and steal fuel with this system in place." Bob straightened and continued to study the tank's discharge structure. "At least not enough to have been used in the fire. There was a lot used as the accelerant."

"So the person had to have bought it, yes?"

Bob narrowed his eyes as he stared at the warehouse. "Or had available access to the tanks."

The implication came across loud and clear. Either the arsonist had to buy the fuel, or got it free from Terrence.

Like his son could.

Talk about tangled nerves. Monique's were in macramé-sized knots.

Her morning had been rushed with arranging to have her new house cleaned. She'd had to pay double to ensure the job was completed by noon, but it was worth it to her. From there, she checked on the furniture she'd ordered originally for the old Pittman place. Thankfully, the warehouses hadn't had a chance to deliver it all before the fire. Now, it was set to be delivered to her new home before three. She'd also switched her utilities to the new house and was assured everything would be on immediately, and finally had gone shopping with Felicia to buy linens, curtains and dishes. And clothes. All in all, she'd accomplished a lot this morning.

She should've been pleased and excited, and she was, but as she followed Felicia into the diner, nerves got the best of her.

Luc and CoCo had returned to Lagniappe, and were meeting them for lunch. Felicia had brought them up to speed on Monique, her relationship to them, the fire and purchasing Justin's house. Now she would meet them for the first time.

Would they accept her as openly as Felicia had? Or would they be cautious, suspicious? Would Luc resent her? Hate that she'd bought the house where he'd almost been murdered?

The door opened and Felicia shrieked and wove quickly around tables.

Monique's mouth went dry as north Louisiana in August. She forced her feet to move and follow Felicia, who hugged a tall, handsome man and an exotic beauty of a woman. Monique stood to the side, actually experiencing the love and security wrapping around the small group.

Never before had she felt like such an outsider, wanting so much to belong.

Felicia turned, putting her arm around Monique's waist and drawing her into the group. "Luc, CoCo, this is our cousin, Monique." She grinned. "This goofy fella is my brother, Luc, and this gorgeous woman is my sister-in-law, CoCo."

Monique smiled shyly. "Hi."

CoCo peered at her from beneath long, luscious lashes. Her dark hair cascaded in long ringlets down her back. A second passed. Then another. Then another. Finally she spoke. "Welcome to the family, Monique." She wrapped graceful arms around Monique's neck and hugged her tight.

Luc gently nudged his wife back. "Stop hogging her." He kissed the top of CoCo's head, grinning at Monique. "Welcome." He pulled her into his strong arms and gave her a bear hug.

Such love and acceptance…it'd been a long time since she felt so surrounded by those emotions. Nothing had moved her so strongly since the first church service after Kent had been killed. The sermon had reached in and touched her very soul, despite her grief. But then she'd had to plan and endure his funeral, and her church family had begun to walk on eggshells around her, making her feel uncomfortable.

And she'd become increasingly angry with God.

"Come, sit, *Boo*. I want to get to know you." CoCo grabbed her hand and tugged her into the chair between her and Luc.

"Boo?" Monique sat, confusion muddling her mind.

Felicia laughed. "It's a Cajun term of endearment. Like *cher*."

"Oh. Hadn't heard that one before."

Luc chuckled as he and Felicia took their seats. "You'll have to forgive us. The eldest of our siblings, we tend to call them all '*Boo*.'"

Tears threatened to shimmer in her eyes. She swallowed hard.

"What does Deputy Anderson have to say about finding the arsonist?" Luc's eyes grew darker, if that was possible.

She told them about Bob Costigan and his questions. "I don't know more than that, I'm afraid." The wheels of justice always moved in the slowest gear possible.

"I wish Bubba was here. He'd take care of this and keep you informed." Luc's jaw set strongly.

"Bubba?"

CoCo laughed. "That's the sheriff, my brother-in-law. He's married to my youngest sister."

"His name is Bubba? Really?" Monique couldn't get over that.

"His real name is René, but only Tara is brave enough to call him that to his face." CoCo chuckled.

"Yeah, if he were here, we'd know exactly what was happening in the investigation," Luc said.

"He and Bubba are friends," CoCo whispered.

"Oh, Gary's been wonderful. I don't think anyone could be handling this any better." Why Monique felt as if she had to defend him, she couldn't figure. The words snuck out before she could stop them.

"Gary?" CoCo raised her eyebrows.

Felicia nudged her sister-in-law. "He's been very, uh, attentive to this case. Even insisted Monique stay with his mother after the threat at Mom's."

"Really?" CoCo faced Monique again. "Do tell."

Heat fanned her face. "There's nothing to tell. He's just doing his job and being nice. That's all."

"Hmm." CoCo winked at her husband. "*Gary's* being nice and doing his job. Isn't that swell?"

Felicia stared at Monique. "Stop. Y'all are embarrassing Monique."

"I'm sorry, *Boo.* I'm only teasing."

"Nothing to apologize for. There's nothing going on." But her heart started an argument with her head on that point. She ignored it.

The waitress appeared, took their orders and withdrew, after paying extra-special attention to Luc. CoCo rolled her eyes. Monique refrained from chuckling, but caught Felicia's under-her-breath giggle.

He turned to her, seriousness covering his handsome features. "I'm very concerned about these threats against you. After the fire…well, it's obvious someone's serious about harming you."

"Do you have any idea who could do such a thing?" CoCo asked.

Monique explained to them about Kent's murder, and Investigator Walkin's reaction to Gary's questions.

Luc nodded. "Good, he's following through on every angle." He paused as the waitress delivered their drinks, then went on as soon as she left. "Of course, someone local has to be involved, to have set the fire."

She'd already considered that. It should have frightened her more, but it didn't. She would stand firm. Especially now, when she had a family to accept her. "I'm ready to put it behind me and get on with my life."

Felicia launched into details of their productive morning. CoCo oohed and aahed over the description of furniture and things purchased. At the end of the conversation, Felicia directed her comments to her brother. "And we need to meet with the Trahan lawyer. Monique is a legal heir of Uncle Justin's, and we need to make sure she gets what she's entitled to from the estate."

"I don't want anything. Really." She let her gaze rest on each person at the table. "I didn't come here for anything but to meet each of you and get to know you. That's it." She didn't want anything of Justin's, not after his rude rejection of her. Besides, having a family was more than enough for her.

"Oh, we know you don't expect or want anything, but it's rightfully yours," Felicia said. "If Uncle Justin had been the man he should've been, you would've had it to begin with."

"I just wanted to know my family." Sobs caught in her chest. "And you've all been so accepting and wonderful…that's all I could ever want." Or need. How long had she envied friends back in Monroe with big families? Now, she had one of her own, and she wouldn't allow anything or anyone to intrude.

"But don't you see, it's not enough for us." Luc took her hand. "We have plenty of money—giving you a share of the estate is the right thing to do. We can't not do it. That'd be wrong of us."

Tears pushed into her eyes. "I don't need money, either. I got a large life insurance policy payout after Kent's death." It seemed so wrong to profit off the loss of her husband, but she'd known he'd wanted to make sure she was provided for.

"If you don't let us do this, it hurts us." Felicia waited until the waitress delivered their food and scurried off again before finishing. "It's not about the money. It's about doing what's right. God tells us to do what's right, regardless."

"But that's not why I came here."

"No one said it was." Luc squeezed her hand. "Let me put this another way…if the tables were turned, and you found out your mother had another child and you met her, wouldn't you feel it was the right thing to do to ensure that a sibling of yours got part of your mother's estate?"

She'd never thought about it like that before. But still…

"We have to do this, Monique. If you decide you want to give your part of the estate away to charity, that's your decision, but you can't expect us not to do what we know is right." Felicia smiled, love pouring from her eyes.

"What do you do with your parts of the estate? I mean, you said it's in a trust or something, right?"

"We use Grandfather's lawyer, who keeps the entire estate in a trust of sorts. We make large contributions to specific charities each year. If one of us needs something, we have the trust write us a check." Felicia shrugged. "Stuff like that."

"And we have specific accounts set up for our future children," Luc added.

An idea came to her. "Why can't I just be added to the estate trust? I don't want to pull anything out, and it sounds like y'all have it set up so well."

Felicia smiled brightly. "That's perfect." She looked at her brother. "Luc?"

He nodded. "I'll call the lawyer tomorrow."

CoCo let out a loud sigh. "Good. That's settled. Can we eat now? I'm starving."

Chuckles rose from around the table.

"Yep. Let me offer grace first, if you can stave off your appetite for a few minutes more," Luc teased.

CoCo reached behind Monique to pop him playfully on the arm. "Always jumping up to do the glory." She addressed Monique. "Forgive my husband for assuming…he takes this head of household thing way too far. Would you like to say grace?"

"Oh, no. Please, go ahead."

She bowed her head and registered Luc speaking, but his words bounced against her hardened heart. She couldn't get over her anger at God yet. He'd allowed Kent to be taken from her so abruptly, before their lives had really begun. Scripture said the Lord giveth and the Lord taketh away. Well, He'd taken away—both her mother and Kent—but what had He given?

She lifted her head and experienced the strong sense of belonging.

Had He given her a replacement family?

FIFTEEN

Showtime.

Gary got out of the cruiser, Bob trailing him. Together, they made their way up the wooden steps to the address listed on the invoice for Niles Patterson, with Gary taking note of everything he saw.

The house needed a lot of work—paint peeled, porch boards warped, in desperate need of replacement, and windowpanes had spiderweb cracks. The bayou edged along the backyard, pushing its fishy odor around the house to the frontyard. If Niles Patterson had lived here for any length of time, he sure wasn't into home improvement.

Pulling out his badge, Gary knocked on the door. "Mr. Patterson? It's Deputy Anderson with the Vermilion parish sheriff's office."

Shuffling sounds came from the other side of the door. "Just a minute."

The door opened with a creak.

A hulk of a man, approximately forty years old with shaggy hair and thick glasses like Sheriff Theriot used to wear, stared out from the crack. "I'm Niles Patterson. What can I do for you?"

Gary held his badge up for the man to see. "We'd like to ask you a few questions, if we might."

"About what?" Cautious, but not rude.

"About a purchase you made last month of biodiesel fuel."

"What about it?"

Gary swallowed his sigh. "We'd rather discuss this with you inside." He'd like to get a glimpse of the interior of the house. Who knew what clues might lurk inside?

Niles swung open the door. "Come on in."

Not exactly the actions of someone with something to hide. And he didn't speak with a Cajun accent—more of a Southern twang.

Gary followed Niles into his living room and sat on the sofa where the man motioned. Springs jabbed Gary in the lower back. He scooted to the edge amid squeaks. No telling what was under the sofa. Gary really didn't want to think about the possibilities.

Bob stood in the doorway, leaning against the doorjamb. Niles dropped to a well-worn recliner. It sagged under his weight. "What about my purchase?"

"We understand you purchased quite a large amount of the fuel." Gary flipped pages in his little notebook. "Sixty-five gallons, to be exact."

"Yep."

Great, this would be like pulling wisdom teeth. "May I ask what you need that much fuel for?"

"Is it against the law to buy it?"

"No, it's not."

"Then why all the questions?"

"Why avoid answering?" Bob interjected.

Niles shoved hair from his forehead and peered into the arson investigator's face. "I bought the fuel because I'm about to launch a charter fishing service. I can use it in my boat with the adapter kit, and it's cheaper than regular petro."

"Really?" Gary made notes. "How long have you lived here in Lagniappe, Mr. Patterson?"

"Moved here about a month or so ago."

"From where?"

"Lake Charles."

"What brought you to Lagniappe?"

Niles shifted in the chair. It creaked in protest. "Why don't you tell me what this is all about?"

"We're investigating a fire. Now, why did you move to Lagniappe?"

The man's face reddened. "I'm going to get married to a gal who lives here. She refused to move, so I did. We'll be getting hitched the end of next month. She wants me to get my business up and running before so we'll have enough money to take a real honeymoon." Even the tips of his ears turned red.

"Congratulations. Who's the lucky lady?"

"Not that it's any of your business, but MaryEllen Grant."

Gary had to think. He knew the name… Oh, yeah, she worked over at Miller's store. A social wannabe. He nodded and jotted down her name.

"You already to the point in setting up your business that you bought fuel?" Bob asked, pushing off from the doorway.

"Yep." Niles shoved to his feet. "Come on out back. I'll show ya."

They followed him through the house toward the back door. Gary chose his steps carefully, avoiding crushed soda cans and paper napkins fisted into tight wads.

Hopefully, MaryEllen would call for a full remodeling before she said, "I do." At the very least, she needed to demand a thorough cleaning of the place. Dirty dishes crowded the sink, and the stench of spoiled milk permeated the close quarters. Gary hurried outside.

"This here's my boat, the *MaryEllen*. Just bought her two weeks ago and got her all gussied up myself."

Too bad Niles hadn't given as much attention to his house. The boat was polished to a shimmering shine. Four captain's chairs, oversized live bait compartment, six life jackets onboard and a selection of fishing tackle that would make Bass Pro Shops proud. Gary made notes, but Niles seemed legit. No one would invest this much in a boat without hoping to recoup some of the expenses.

"Where are you storing the fuel?" Bob asked.

"Over here." Niles led them to what looked like a propane gas tank. "I recycled this to hold my fuel, so I don't have to keep running over to Fenton's place if I get lucky and charter back-to-back fishing expeditions."

Bob inspected the gauge on the tank. "This reading accurate?"

"Pretty much."

Bob caught Gary's gaze and gave a curt nod.

Time to move on. Gary extended his hand to Niles. "Thank you for your time, Mr. Patterson. Good luck in your business, and your upcoming marriage."

Niles shook his hand. "Thanks."

On the walk around the house to the car—no way was Gary going back through that kitchen—Bob informed him the gauge read almost fifty-four gallons in the tank. "He had to fill up his boat, so that wouldn't leave enough to have been used as the accelerant."

"I'll still run a background check on him, just to be on the safe side." But as Gary started the cruiser's engine, his gut instinct told him the man would come back clean.

"Want to pay Mr. Haynie a visit?"

Gary glanced at the dashboard clock. Four-fifteen. "Actually, I need to check back in at the station, file this report and order the background checks on Patterson and Haynie."

"Yeah, I need to send in my report, too. I'll meet you at the office at eight in the morning. Maybe we can surprise Kevin Haynie."

"I hope so." Gary turned onto the station's street.

Yeah, he really hoped so, because their suspect list was dwindling down to nothing, and he hadn't a clue where else to look.

Where on earth had the rocker come from?

Monique stared as the delivery truck unloaded a single, large wooden rocker with cushion. "Where do you want this?" The man huffed.

She'd tried to find one and order it earlier, but had been out of luck. "Um, I think there's a mistake. I didn't order this."

"Lady, it comes to you. Just tell me where to put it."

Without question, she knew. "The bedroom." She led the way down the hall.

He shifted around her into the room. "Where?"

"By the window." It looked perfect there, just as she'd imagined. "But I didn't order this."

He handed her an envelope and a clipboard. "Sign here." He pointed to a line and stuck a pen in her hand.

So what if she was charged for this later? She'd tried to order one like it anyway, but had been told it wasn't available. The rocker was the exact one she'd wanted.

She scrawled her signature where the man indicated, then handed the clipboard back.

He took it and headed to the front door without so much as "Thank you" or "Have a nice day." She followed and saw him out.

"I thought you couldn't find the chair." Felicia walked into the living room from the kitchen, chewing on a piece of cheese from the tray Parker had brought over earlier.

The guy still gave her the willies, although he'd been nothing but nice.

"They just brought it in," CoCo announced around a cracker.

"But I didn't order it." Monique realized she still held the envelope. Turning it over, she withdrew a card from inside. It was a housewarming card. She slowly opened it.

TO SIT AND LOOK OUT OVER THE BAYOU. CON-GRATULATIONS ON YOUR NEW HOME, GARY.

Tears choked her. "It's a housewarming gift. From Gary."

Both CoCo and Felicia seemed to "hmm" in unison. She

ignored them. How kind of him. To send a gift for the house. Her house. And the perfect gift, too. One she'd mentioned she wanted. He'd paid attention and ordered it for her. Her pulse hiccupped. Such a gesture…well, she'd figure out why her heart pounded so quickly later.

"Wait. I have a housewarming gift for you, too." Felicia nudged her husband. He disappeared outside, returning in a few minutes with a large, framed piece covered with brown paper. He handed it to Felicia, who smiled and put it in Monique's hands. "This is for you. Spence and I saw it and immediately thought of you yesterday."

Monique was overwhelmed. Her new family and friends were so thoughtful and generous.

Family. How many years she'd yearned for family, and now she had an amazing one. A family who loved and accepted her just as she was.

"Well, open it! I want to see what it is." CoCo hopped from foot to foot.

Laughing, Monique ripped the paper and stared at the picture.

Framed in the same cherrywood as the coffee and end tables, it was a portrait. The background of the picture conveyed a sun setting over the bayou. The beautiful photography captured the feel of peace and tranquility Monique had felt immediately upon arriving in the area. Inscribed in black calligraphy was a Scripture verse:

You are my hiding place;
And you will protect me from trouble
And surround me with songs of deliverance.
                                        —Psalms 32:7

Monique stared at Felicia, tears burning the back of her eyes. She blinked several times. "Thank you. It's beautiful."

"Spence and I saw it at the same time and looked at each other and said, 'Monique.' We had to get it for you."

"I love it." She smiled at Spence. "Thank you. Would you hang it over the mantel for me, please?"

"Yes, ma'am. Let me find the hammer and nails." He trotted off toward the garage, which was piled high with furniture boxes and empty shopping bags.

Monique turned slowly around in the living room. Her living room, with furniture she'd picked out while laughing with Felicia. Her home, her family, her place.

All the furniture had been delivered earlier and she, CoCo and Felicia had ordered Luc and Spence around in the arrangement and rearranging. Several men from Spence's congregation had come by to provide muscle. Now, with everyone gone save her family, the house seemed in order, aside from the decor touches she'd add later.

Luc wandered through the house, inspecting.

She paused, watching him move from room to room. What could he be thinking? Was he remembering his great-uncle's things here? Was the memory of the harrowing moment when his uncle had turned on him and tried to kill him haunting him now?

He stepped back into the living room, a smile on his face. "It looks really nice, Monique. It's uniquely you."

Her face muscles quivered into a big grin. "I'm gl—"

Berrk. Berrk. Berrk.

CoCo spun toward the front windows, now boasting new drapes. "What in the world is that?"

"My car alarm." Monique rushed toward the door.

Luc grabbed her arm. "Let me and Spence check it out." They hurried out to the car, Monique hot on their heels, followed by CoCo and Felicia.

No one was around the SUV, or even in sight. Monique went to the keypad on the door and punched in the numbers. The screeching ceased.

Luc sighed. "I thought I told y'all to wait inside."

"And we're so good at obeying, right?" CoCo grinned.

Monique just stared at her vehicle. Her back two tires were flat, having been slit. A note was tucked under the back windshield wiper. A note with one word, made in big, black, block letters.

LEAVE.

"Oh, no," Felicia whimpered.

Spence grabbed his wife and Monique gently by the arms, turning them toward the door. "Get inside." He nodded to Luc, who already had CoCo by the hand. "We'll call the deputy from there."

Monique tugged free of Spence. "Let me get the letter."

"No!" Luc moved to block her path. He lowered his tone. "It's evidence. Gary will need to dust it for prints and such."

Right. She knew that. Just couldn't think clearly at the moment.

Inside the house, Luc bolted the door and grabbed his cell phone. "Spence, watch out the window to make sure you don't see anyone coming back." He moved into the kitchen, his voice asking for Gary filtering through the space.

Felicia and CoCo led Monique to the new sofa. "It'll be okay."

She gulped in a deep breath, held it for long seconds, then released it all slowly. "Yeah, I'm fine."

And she was. But she was also furious.

She stood and joined Spence at the window. She hated hiding in her own house, looking out a draped window.

Who did this guy think he was? She wasn't some mealymouthed, scared-of-her-own-shadow type of gal. She wasn't about to let phone calls and a note scare her away from the new life she'd carefully started constructing.

After burning down her house, did this guy think slit tires and threats had any intimidation power?

"The dispatcher said Deputy Anderson is on his way into the

station now. She said she'll send him right over," Luc announced as he closed his phone and returned to the living room.

"Good. I'm ready for this guy to get caught." Outrage and a sense of helplessness over the situation flooded her veins. She stared out the window, the setting sun casting dancing prisms over the bayou.

So peaceful, yet so menacing at the same time.

SIXTEEN

Had the chair been delivered yet?

What Gary wouldn't give to have seen the look of surprise on Monique's face when the rocker she'd wanted and couldn't get showed up. He'd had to pull a lot of strings to get the sales force at the furniture store to tell her they were out of stock and even unable to sell the display model. He hoped it had made her happy. She didn't have nearly enough happiness in her life.

If she'd only return to God, contentment could be hers. He knew firsthand that just because you walked with Christ didn't mean you had it easier. Not hardly. Truth be told, he figured it was harder because of the striving to do what's right all the time. Probably because Christians tried to do it all on their own strength, instead of relying on God's. But, as Gary reminded himself, this earth was not home for Christians. It was the promise of eternal life that brought such contentment in a Christian's soul.

It wasn't as if Monique didn't believe in God—she'd said she was mad at Him. Maybe now was the time to witness to her more, to help her see she needed to talk to God and work out her feelings.

He silently prayed for just that as he dropped Bob off at the motel, then headed to the station. It'd been a long day, and the stress weighed down his every muscle. Maybe he'd even put off making out his report.

Missy wasn't at her station as he made his way toward the office. He went to his office, slumped into the chair and ordered the background checks on Patterson and Haynie. Maybe they'd get lucky and one of them would have a rap sheet, although he doubted it about Patterson. Probably not on Haynie either, but he could still hope.

Carrying the paperwork to have Missy process first thing, he glanced through the reports Mike had filed for the past two weeks: drunk and disorderly, teenage DUI, domestic disturbance, violation of leash law, robbery—whoa, the homeowner who made the report was one Kevin Haynie. Gary pulled the report and hotfooted it back to Mike's desk. The rookie deputy should still be in the office.

Sure enough, Mike sat in the metal rolling chair, closing down the computer. "Hey, how's your day been?"

Gary waved the report. "Brief me on this, please." He sat on the edge of the desk.

Mike took the papers and scanned them. "Yeah. Mr. Haynie called in a report that his shed was trashed. Heard some noise out there one night, but didn't think it was anything more than a coon until he went to get a shovel out of there the next morning."

Gary mentally backtracked. "He's stating this theft occurred on, um…"

"Last Wednesday night. He called and reported it on Thursday morning." Mike ran a thumb under his chin. "We've been backed up, so I only got around to filing the report today."

"You went and interviewed him?"

Mike shot him a quizzical look. "Well, yeah. That's policy, yes?"

"It's just this man is someone I'm set to go talk to tomorrow about the arson case." Gary proceeded to fill Mike in on the details of his day.

"Wow. This is really odd." Mike glanced back over the report. "Reported missing along with a battery charger and voltage tester was a twenty-five-gallon container of biodiesel fuel."

Something didn't feel right.

"What was his attitude like when you talked to him? His body language?"

Mike ran a hand over his hair. "Nothing that triggered any questions in my mind, but then again, I only filed the report. He gave a pretty concise account."

Something was still off about the situation. "I'll see what I can figure out tomorrow morning when I visit him." Gary lifted the report. "At least now I have an additional reason to talk to him."

"Want me to go with you?"

"Nah. Bob Costigan, the arson investigator, will join me. I need you to hold down the fort again."

"No problem."

"Deputy Anderson," Missy's voice shrieked. "I didn't know you'd come back in yet. I've been trying to reach you in the cruiser."

"What is it, Missy?"

"Luc Trahan called. Said to tell you to get out to Monique Harris's new place. Her tires have been slit and there's a letter."

How long ago had the call come in? Why hadn't Monique called his cell?

"I'm on my way."

"Want me to assist?" Mike stood, his hand on his belt rig.

Why not? If Gary didn't make chief deputy, he at least wanted the man who got the promotion to know what he was doing. "Come on. You can follow me in your cruiser."

"Missy, radio me if you need me."

"Will do." She popped her gum, which annoyed him all the more. One of these days…

Off daylight saving time, dusk settled over Lagniappe. The cool evening caused a low-lying fog to hover just over the road.

Not wanting to turn on the lights and siren in the event they would draw even more attention to Monique, Gary still raced through the town toward her home. She hadn't bothered to call him. She'd had Luc call the station. What did that say about her belief in his investigative abilities?

He dialed Luc's cell phone number and waited. As soon as Luc answered, he proceeded to get the information about what had transpired.

Two rights and one left turn later, his tires sang against Wyatt Lane. Mike's low beams flashed in the rearview. Gary slowed and pulled into Monique's driveway. He resisted the urge to slam his foot on the accelerator. Calm and cool, that's what his position dictated. But his heart wouldn't stop racing until he saw Monique was okay with his own eyes.

He parked about ten feet behind her Expedition. Every light in the house blazed, spilling out into the night. Leaving his headlights on, he grabbed the crime scene kit from the trunk. Mike appeared at his side, slipping on latex gloves.

The job had to come first, despite the desire to run to the house and see Monique for himself. Gary opened the case, donned gloves and passed the digital camera to Mike.

The back tires of the SUV had been slit. Had to be with a knife. He pulled out a ruler and measured the slits, noting the measurements in his notebook. Mike clicked away with the camera, the flashes coming so rapidly, it nearly made Gary want to scream.

Finally, the front door opened and Monique stood bathed in the backlight from the foyer. His breath caught in his throat. As if time was moving frame by frame, he slowly straightened, his feet planted into the gravel.

She descended the steps with the Trahan group behind her, but Gary only had eyes for her. Her cheeks were tinged with pink. Her coppery hair flew around her head as the wind picked up. The closer she came, the quicker his heart thumped.

Oh, no. Heart racing at her mere presence. Dizzy when she smiled at him. Urge to protect her no matter what the cost. She'd moved well beyond a victim of a crime and crept closely around the edges of his heart.

Father God, help me. I think I'm falling for her, and I know I can't. I shouldn't. Please give me wisdom and guidance. I'm not strong enough to withstand this alone.

As she drew closer, he noticed something else about her…her eyes, which were shimmering almost an emerald color.

Anger. The woman was madder than a wet hen.

"Can you believe he had the nerve to do this?" She stood mere inches from him. Fury radiated from her like heat around a *cochon de lait*. "The first night at my house, he does this?"

He grabbed her flailing arm, pulling her toward him. She looked into his eyes, and he hoped reassurance—nothing more—shone in his expression. "We're going to do everything we can to catch him. I promise you that."

"He's acting very fast on his threats. It's only my first night."

"You had your utilities turned on. Your deed was filed at the courthouse. You ordered furniture delivered. All flashing neon lights to him."

"It makes me so mad. He's trying to scare me off. Well, I'm not leaving." She crossed her arms over her chest and stomped her foot.

He avoided Spence and Luc's grins, sure she'd go ballistic if she caught him laughing at her. But it was hard to resist. "We're going to process the evidence and see where it leads." He nodded to Mike. "Go ahead and bag the letter."

As Mike moved to do just that, Gary took Monique a few steps away from her vehicle. "Did you get any calls today? Any other types of threats? Anything unusual?"

"No, my phone service won't be on until tomorrow. But I didn't get anything on my cell."

"It's harder to get those numbers." He glanced over her head to see Mike slipping the letter into a large envelope. "Go ahead and radio for a tow truck to take the Expedition."

"You're taking my truck?"

"Evidence. He might've touched the glass, or the side panel by the tires. We'll dust everything."

"Great. So I'm without a vehicle now?"

"I'm afraid so. It should only take us a day or two."

"First he takes my house, now my truck." She clenched her hands into tight little fists.

"Monique, I need you to calm down for a minute and think. Did you have any visitors today, aside from your family?"

"Delivery people from the furniture store and some people from Spence's church. Oh, and Parker dropped by earlier with a cheese and cracker tray."

Gary froze. "Estimated time between his leaving and your car alarm going off?"

She shrugged. "I don't know. An hour or so, maybe. Why?"

"Just making sure I have everything down right."

"That's about it."

"Okay. I need you and everyone to go back into the house. Mike and I will finish up out here, then come in to take everyone's statements."

She hesitated, looking past him to Mike and his flashing camera.

"Monique? We have to do our job."

"Fine. Do your job." She spun and marched back toward the porch. Felicia ran after her and CoCo, too, but not before she tossed Gary a disgusted look.

"What?" Gary looked to Luc.

Luc and Spence both chuckled.

"What?"

"You've got a crush on her, don't you?" Spence asked.

There that heat came again, spreading across his neck. Good thing it was night out. "Please. I'm just doing my job."

Both of the other men laughed.

"Yeah, that's what I said, too." Spence clapped him on the shoulder. "Good luck. She's a live one." He headed toward the house.

"Really. I'm just doing my job."

Luc shook his head. "Keep telling yourself that, okay?" He followed the preacher into the house.

Gary exhaled sharply. If those two could see his feelings so easily, had Monique?

Please, no.

* * *

How could she be attracted to such an infuriating man?

Seriously? Gary had all but patted her on her head and sent her on her merry little way, as if she were a child.

Wait a minute—had she just admitted to herself that she was attracted to him? That stopped her fuming.

She paused, letting her mind wrap around the realization, waiting for the guilt to come.

Seconds ticked by. The guilt never came. Matter of fact, only exhilaration filled her after her acknowledgment.

She was attracted to Gary Anderson, and she didn't feel guilty about it. Didn't feel as if she were cheating on Kent.

What was happening to her?

Stress, that had to be it. Her mind and emotions were playing tricks on her because of everything that was happening. Yeah, that's the ticket.

"Here, have some hot tea." Felicia put a cup into her hands.

Monique took a sip, nearly scalding her tongue. She set the cup on the linen place mat she'd carefully picked out today. She loved it. Loved everything about her house and the day she'd spent decorating it.

No, she wouldn't allow some faceless man to invade *her* space. Make her jumpy in her own home. She'd vowed to stick it out, to stand on her own, and that's exactly what she would do.

She crossed to the kitchen island and opened the cabinet.

"What're you doing, *Boo?*"

She plopped the Vermilion parish phone book onto the counter with a thud, grabbed a notepad and pen from beside the phone, and boosted herself onto the bar stool. "I'm going to get numbers for a security system company, a surveillance company and the pound."

CoCo smiled. "I get the security system and surveillance, but the pound?"

"I'm going to adopt a dog."

Laughing, CoCo clapped her hands. "Oh, *Boo,* I'm so glad you're in our family. You fit right in."

"How's that?" She chewed on the cap of the pen.

"Because you're headstrong and stubborn, just like the other women in this family," Luc said, but winked at his wife.

"I prefer determined and strong, thank you very much." CoCo angled her head in that distinct way of hers.

"We'll never win, Luc. Just give it up." Spence moved behind his wife and kissed her temple.

"Like you want to win at something?" Felicia giggled and then looked at Monique. She sobered immediately. "I'm sorry. We're joking around at a very stressful time for you."

"Nonsense. I'm not scared. This jerk isn't going to bring my life to a screeching halt. I won't stand for it." Not anymore. She'd passed the point where she'd allow her life to be run by anyone else.

"You go, sistah." CoCo raised a fist into the air.

Luc shook his head. "I give up. Too much estrogen in one room for me." He pointed a finger at Monique. "But regardless of how tough you are, I'm going to camp out on your new sofa tonight."

"I can't let you do that."

CoCo jumped in. "You have to. Otherwise, he'll bother me all night, worrying about you."

Monique chewed her bottom lip.

"I'll be gone well before daylight." Luc grinned and winked before turning to his brother-in-law. "Spence, I'm going into the living room to wait on the deputy."

"I'm with you, man." Spence planted another kiss on Felicia's temple before following Luc from the kitchen.

"Seriously, we didn't mean to make light of everything happening to you." Felicia fluffed her honey-colored hair.

"No problem. I refuse to let all of that drag me down. I'm not going to react anymore. I'm going to be proactive. I'm going to take a stand. This jerk wants to mess with me, I'm going to stand up for myself."

"Good for you. I understand one hundred percent." CoCo slipped onto an opposite bar stool. "And we're behind you one hundred percent."

"I'll call these places first thing in the morning. I'm not gonna play around with this guy."

"Be careful, Monique." Felicia's face was wreathed in worry. "He's already tried to kill you by burning down your house."

"And he makes threatening phone calls and leaves anonymous letters. The man's a coward." Monique finished writing down the numbers and snapped the phone book closed. "I don't do cowards."

The front door slammed. "Monique?"

Gary. And he didn't sound very happy with her. She pushed off the stool. "In here. The kitchen."

His steps treaded heavily on the polished wooden floor. He entered the kitchen, brandishing a gun in a holster. "This was in your truck. Care to explain why you're driving around with a concealed weapon?"

SEVENTEEN

She felt like a teenager caught sneaking in after curfew.

And she hated the sensation because she had no reason to feel like that. She had every right to have that gun—now more than ever.

Felicia and CoCo discreetly slipped out of the kitchen.

Monique crossed her arms and cocked her head. "Because I have a permit to carry it—concealed, by the way."

Gary set the gun on the counter. "How's that? It didn't come up on the background check."

"Because I haven't committed any crimes, and that's all those checks report. My husband was a private investigator. I was his assistant. He and I both qualified on the range and got permits."

"You pack a Desert Eagle?" Gary's eyes were wide. But with what? Admiration or intimidation? So many men had a problem with women being crack shots. And she was an ace.

"Yep. I also have a Beretta and a nine mil in the closet. And before you ask, I have permits for those, too."

"Quite an arsenal you have there."

"Kent and I enjoyed target shooting. We even won several competitions." And she proudly had the blue ribbons to prove it.

Well, she did before the fire consumed them all.

"I never knew a woman to enjoy firearms."

"Well, now you have." She wished she didn't sound so snarky, but he brought her defensive hackles to attention.

"You know I'll have to ask you to see that permit."

"Of course." She jerked her purse off the counter and flipped through her wallet. Sure he had to ask—he was all about the job again. She thrust the permit toward him.

He took it, studied it a moment, then handed it back. "Okay."

"So, instead of asking me about a weapon I have legally in my possession, why don't you go out and find this jerk who seems obsessed with harassing me?" She put the permit back in her purse, followed by the holstered gun.

Hurt marched across his face.

The deputy Gary had brought with him chose that moment to enter the kitchen. "Excuse me, ma'am. Gary, tow truck's here."

"Have them load up her vehicle and take it to impound." He spoke to the deputy, but kept his gaze focused on Monique.

"Um, I came to get the keys."

She reached into her purse again and retrieved her key ring. She removed the key to the truck and handed it to the other deputy. "Here."

"We'll let you know when you can pick it up, ma'am." He turned to Gary. "Want me to head back to the station and fill out the lab forms on the vehicle?"

"Yeah. Thanks, Mike."

He nodded at Gary, then Monique. "G'night, ma'am."

If he called her ma'am one more time…

"Look, I know you're upset. You have every right to be. But I'm doing my job as best I can. I want to catch this guy just as much as you do." Gary stood straighter, taller.

"I'm sure you do. You police officers always do. Looks good on your records." Why couldn't she just keep her mouth shut?

"Have I done something wrong here, Monique? Anybody would ask to see your permit. You know that."

And she did.

She blew the bangs off her forehead. "I'm sorry. I wish I could explain why I'm always snapping at you." Maybe because she was attracted to him and felt bad because she *didn't* feel guilty about that, which triggered the snarkiness.

"It's okay. You're stressed. A lot's happened over the last couple of weeks."

"It feels like months. But I shouldn't keep biting your head off. I'm really sorry." She ducked her head. She really was sorry. "And I haven't even thanked you for the rocker."

He lifted her chin with his thumb until she looked in him the eye. "You just did. You're welcome."

Her heart wouldn't stop doing flips. Her breath came in spurts. Even her head felt dizzy, like she'd just stepped off a roller coaster.

His gaze remained locked on hers as he slowly bent forward. He tilted his head slightly. She gave a quick intake of breath just before his lips brushed over hers. Not really a kiss. Not really. More like the promise of a kiss to come. A hint.

One that left her breathless and wanting another.

He straightened and cleared his throat. "I need to go question the others. Get their, uh, statements." His normally smooth voice sounded hoarse.

She nodded, not taking her eyes off his.

"Well, I'll, uh, go talk to her. Them. Them in the living room." He took a step backward, away from her. "And arrange for protection for you starting tomorrow. Luc said he's staying here tonight?"

"Yes. Okay." Her voice sounded too falsetto to her own ears. She cleared her throat. "Yes. Of course."

"Monique?"

"Yes?" Her reply came out almost on top of his saying her name. Her pulse reverberated in her temples.

"Would you have supper with me tomorrow night? Not to discuss this case, or anything? Just you and me, having supper, together?"

Her heart did a triple back handspring. "Are you asking me out on a date, Deputy Anderson?"

"I guess I am." He grinned. "Are you interested?"

She couldn't contain her responding smile. "Sounds like a date to me."

"I'll pick you up around five, then?"

"Yes."

He paused, staring at her. Then grabbed his notebook and pencil from his pocket. "I'm going to talk to them now."

"Okay."

Turning, he nearly ran smack into the counter. He sidestepped and headed into the living room.

Alone, Monique's heartbeat echoed inside her head. Had she just accepted a date from him?

She smiled. Oh, yeah, she had.

Even better? She was looking forward to it. Very much.

Thursday morning dawned clear and crisp over the bayou. Not cold—it never was in Lagniappe—but chilly enough to warrant a jacket. Beautiful weather, beautiful nature, beautiful everything.

Gary grinned as he drove to the station. He waved at passing townsfolk, smiled at people out walking their dogs before going to work. Luc had called at daylight and said there'd been no further activity at Monique's house. She was safe and secure. It was a glorious day.

Then again, maybe his great mood was because he had a date with Monique tonight.

He pulled into the sheriff's office parking lot, whistling under his breath, and strode across the lot. He had a busy morning planned, and he'd better get his head out of the clouds and focus on the job at hand. That's why he'd come in so early.

With only the night dispatcher still on duty and reading at the front desk, the station was quiet. Gary finished his reports and filed the new ones. He reviewed the lab order for Monique's truck, impressed at the thoroughness of Mike's instructions. The man was a good deputy. Might even be a good chief deputy, as much as the thought pained Gary.

With everything that'd happened in their small little town over the past couple of years, the citizens of Lagniappe deserved the best officer for chief deputy. If that happened to be Mike, so be it. Gary would find other ways to help his mother.

But Gary had to admit he'd be sorely disappointed if he wasn't promoted.

"You 'bout ready to head over to Haynie's place?"

The booming voice caused Gary to jump and turn simultaneously.

Bob stood in the hallway, chuckling. "Didn't mean to scare ya."

So the old codger *could* laugh. Would wonders never cease? Gary shook his head and strode toward the front door. He told the dispatcher to let Missy and Mike know where he'd be, then headed to the cruiser. On the drive to Kevin Haynie's house, he told Bob about the break-in report filed by Mr. Haynie last week, handing him a copy of the report.

Bob grunted as he read. "Sounds like this could be the source of the accelerant, but if it was stolen, then we're back to square one."

"I know." Still, he refused to be discouraged. They *would* find this guy. And when they did…

"Did you get the check back on these characters?"

"No. They should come in sometime this morning."

"Maybe that'll give us another starting point."

"Hope so." Man, did he ever.

Bob read off the directions to the Haynie property. Gary eased up to the house, parking the car in front of a manufactured home. With white siding and green trim, the house needed the kudzu cut back and the windows washed, but it was in good condition. Couldn't be more than five years old at most. Last Gary had heard, the Sanderson family still owned the place and rented it out. He'd check on that.

A Ford sedan, about three years old, sat alone under the carport. No bikes, ATVs or motorcycles crowded the area.

The house stood on the opposite side of town from Monique's new place. The property butted up against the bayou, but then again, most of the land in Lagniappe did. Unlike Patterson's place, this yard looked well-kept. At least the lawn was mowed. The little porch looked as if the wood had been treated in the fall.

Gary knocked on the door, pulling his badge.

"Qui ici?" came the reply from the other side.

"Deputy Anderson with the Vermilion parish sheriff's office."

The door opened and Gary had to look down to meet the man's eyes. "I need to speak to Kevin Haynie, please."

"I'm Kevin. How can I help you?"

The man couldn't be more than five feet and had the slightest frame. Although Gary knew from the break-in report Mr. Haynie was forty-eight, he had boyish features that made him look at least a decade younger.

"I'm Deputy Anderson—" he flashed his badge "—and I need to follow up on the theft report you filed."

"Most certainly. *Tout de suite.*" He waved Gary and Bob into the living room. "Please, have a seat."

The room held a sofa, a love seat and a recliner. Really, too much furniture for the small space, but nice pieces. A coffee table crowded the arrangement even further. The smell of incense burned Gary's nostrils as he sat on the edge of the sofa. As he had at Niles Patterson's, Bob stood in the doorway while Mr. Haynie perched in the recliner that seemed too big for his frame.

Gary pulled out his pen and notebook. "According to the report you filed, Mr. Haynie, twenty-five gallons of biodiesel was stolen from your shed last Wednesday night. Is that correct?"

"Yes. My battery charger and voltage meter were stolen, as well. That meter was brand-new, too. Only used once."

"May I ask why you had twenty-five gallons of biodiesel? You purchased that about two and a half weeks ago from Un-Bio-Believable, right?"

The man wriggled closer to the edge of the chair. "I did, yes."

"Why?" Bob boomed from the doorway.

Mr. Haynie did a little start, twisting to stare at the hulking arson investigator. "To be honest, I wanted to test the fuel. Break down the components."

"For what purpose?" Bob took a step into the room.

"Well, with gas prices the way they are, I wanted to see if I could duplicate the fuel and produce it myself."

"For personal use?" Gary kept writing in his notebook, noting Haynes's Cajun dialect.

"Mainly." Haynie's cheeks reddened. "But if I could duplicate it, I could also make some to sell to some of the locals."

"How long have you lived here, Mr. Haynie?" Gary tapped the pen against paper.

"About a month or so, I'd guess."

"You bought this place?"

"Renting it." He rolled his eyes. "Do you really think I'd decorate like this?" He gestured toward the duck hunting scene hanging prominently on the wall.

"Why are you in Lagniappe, Mr. Haynie?"

The man scooted back against the chair. "What a rude question, Deputy."

"I don't mean to pry, but I need to clarify the details for the report."

"Well, I'm a bit of a vagabond, a gypsy, if you will. I meet a lot of interesting people as I move about. I sometimes go to places I've been told about. See what the draw is."

"Why?" Bob asked from his sentry post.

"Because I'm working on a novel. But Louisiana is my home— I'm from Lafayette originally."

"Pardon me if this seems like another rude question, but how do you afford to live?" Gary asked.

Haynie shrugged. "I do a little part-time work here and there. Freelance. Dabble in the stock market a bit. I manage to keep myself afloat. But that's why I rent and don't buy, Deputy."

"Are you working anywhere here?"

"Not yet. As I said, I've only been here a month or so."

Very strange that the two new customers of Fenton's both had moved to town recently. And both came to town right before Monique did.

"Can we see the shed?" Bob asked.

"Of course." Haynie jumped up and led them to the back door.

The little shed sat perpendicular between the house and the bayou. This property, unlike so many others in the row of homes, had a decent-sized backyard, and no boat dock or pier. The outbuilding, in the same white siding as the house, had a single, sliding door.

Haynie gestured to the closing. "There was a padlock here, but they tore it right off." He shook his head.

Gary stared at the area. Sure enough, the flimsy metal had been contorted so a lock could be removed. He slipped on a pair of gloves and tested the density of the metal. Weak. Even a kid in middle school could've broken into the shed.

He slid the door open. Sunlight flooded the space, reflecting the little particles dancing in the air. No stale stench assaulted his senses, however. Only a subtle undertone of grease.

A manual lawn mower sat on one side of the building, while hand tools hung on a Peg-Board on the opposite side of the wall, with an empty worktable beneath.

Haynie motioned to the table. "That's where the diesel and battery charger were." He pointed to a vacancy on the Peg-Board. "And that's where the voltage meter hung."

Gary studied the table. No layer of dust coated the top, which meant no outlines of a gas container or battery charger were visible.

"How did you keep the fuel stored?" Bob asked, inching his massive shoulders into the cramped space.

"In one of those red, double gas cans." Haynie gave a nervous cough. "Well, I don't know why they're still called cans. They're plastic."

Bob gave a noncommittal grunt. "How were you doing the testing on the fuel?"

"I hadn't started yet. That was my future project, to set things up."

"You know, Mr. Haynie, I'm just a sheriff's deputy, so forgive me if this question seems elementary, but wouldn't you have to have some sort of chemistry background to break down and analyze the fuel for duplication purposes?"

"No, not at all." The man's eyes flickered. "Right now, over the Internet, you can order all kinds of kits and testing systems. They come with detailed instructions. Just last month, I was able to duplicate the refinement of certain battery acids and build my own rechargeable batteries."

Still sounded like Greek to Gary.

"Why would you store fuel so close to a battery charger?" Bob interrupted the chemistry lesson.

The excitement fled from Haynie's face. "It was unplugged. Why wouldn't I?"

"Because fuel is, I don't know—flammable? And a battery charger? Even my mother would know to keep the two apart."

"Well, I didn't even think about it. Besides, once I began my testing of the fuel, I would've had to move the charger anyway."

Bob grunted again, but said no more.

"I think that's all for now, Mr. Haynie." Gary pulled off his glove with a pop and shoved it into his pocket. He held out a business card. "If you think of anything else that could be important, please give me a call."

"Sure will. Thank you, deputies."

Gary didn't bother to correct Haynie. Better if the man didn't realize Bob wasn't on the force.

Back in the car, Bob cracked the window. "Strange little man, wouldn't you say?"

"I think he comes across that way because of his stature."

"Or lack thereof." Bob shook his head. "Still, something's not right about him. I'll be interested in seeing his background report."

"Me, too."

But as he turned into the sheriff's office parking lot, Gary had to admit he was more interested in seeing Monique on their date.

He needed to make sure he didn't let himself fall, though. Not while her relationship with God was unresolved.

If only his heart would listen.

EIGHTEEN

The lawyer must cost a fortune.

Monique sat flanked by Felicia and Luc in the very lush conference room of the Hudson Law Firm. For such a little town, Lagniappe sure had an abundance of attorneys.

She shifted in the leather chair. The rollers stuck against the plush carpet. She let out a long breath, unease settling between her shoulder blades, still not sure if she was doing the right thing.

"How'd you sleep last night?" Felicia asked.

"Fine, once I fell asleep." Monique forced a little laugh. "But the security company came out first thing this morning and installed my new alarm system. It's pretty cool. They left right before the car company delivered my rental."

"Good. I'm sure you feel better now that you have the security system and wheels, yes?"

"And I'm still going to adopt a dog when I leave here."

Luc opened his mouth, but was cut off by the door swinging open with a muted whoosh.

An elderly, distinguished-looking man with gray hair waltzed in and took the head chair. "Sorry I'm running a little late." He set down his attaché case. "Good morning, Felicia and Luc. And you must be Monique? I'm Marshall Hudson, legal monitor of the Trahan estate trust."

"Monique Harris. Nice to meet you."

"Let's get down to business, shall we?" He withdrew a file from his case and perused the information. "Now, let me make sure I have this right—Monique, you've discovered you're the biological child of Justin Trahan?"

"Yes."

"Do you have proof of this?"

She swallowed the lump caught in her throat. "Yes. We had a saliva DNA paternity test performed well over six months ago. The test is ninety-eight percent accurate."

"Good." He nodded and made notes with his Cross pen. "I'll need a copy of that, for the files, of course."

"It might take me a little while to obtain copies."

"Oh?" He glanced up and removed his wire-rimmed glasses, shoving the end of the earpiece into his mouth.

"Her house burned down with everything inside," Luc offered.

"Ah. Well, just contact the testing company and request a copy." He looked back to the file and made additional notations.

"Yes, sir." Sheesh, he made her feel like she was in elementary school and had been sent to the principal's office.

"Luc and Felicia, you aren't contesting this, correct?"

"Of course not." Felicia tossed her slick hair over her shoulder.

Mr. Hudson smiled. "I just have to ask, you understand."

"We're not contesting," Luc affirmed.

"Good." The lawyer flipped pages in the file. "It will be no problem to add Ms. Harris to the fund as an equal shareholder."

"That's what we want." Felicia patted Monique's knee under the table.

"Now, there is a question about the special trust fund." He lifted his gaze to Monique, and set his glasses on the table. "After we receive the documentation on the paternity test, we'll need you to decide what you want to do with those funds."

"What're you talking about?" Monique looked from the lawyer to her cousins. "I don't understand."

"Neither do I." Luc swiveled his chair toward Mr. Hudson. "What special trust fund?"

"You don't know? I was sure your grandfather had told you…" The lawyer flipped through more pages in the file. "Ah, here it is. Almost four decades ago, Beau Trahan contacted this firm and requested a special trust fund be created for any heirs that came forward with legal proof of paternity by his brother, Justin Trahan."

"I had no clue." Felicia looked across Monique to her brother. "Luc, did Grandfather ever tell you this?"

"No."

"Well, it states that in the event legal proof is provided to establish an heir of Justin Trahan's, that heir is entitled to the full amount set aside in the special trust fund. If more than one heir is established, they are to split the fund equally."

"This is separate from the Trahan estate trust?" Luc asked.

"Of course. Your grandfather set this up to protect any children Justin might have."

Luc tented his hands over the table and leaned forward. "What happens if no heirs come forward?"

"According to the draft drawn upon Beau's request, if no heir presented legal proof of Justin's paternity by the time Justin turned seventy-five, then the funds would revert to Justin independent of any of the funds held in trust by this law firm."

"And what would happen to the money if no heir came forward and he was incarcerated at the time the trust matured?"

Glancing back over the paperwork, Mr. Hudson hesitated. "Well, I suppose we'd have to double-check the legalities, but it would either be held in Justin's name until death or release, or it would revert back into the Trahan estate trust."

"How much is in this fund?" Felicia squeezed Monique's knee.

Mr. Hudson slipped his glasses back on and peered at the file. "As of the end of last quarter, just last month, the fund's balance was over two million dollars."

* * *

Well, well, well. The self-proclaimed vagabond Kevin Haynie sure had failed to tell Gary about his stay in a Louisiana federal penitentiary. Gary would just bet the man got plenty of fodder for his novel there.

He tugged the rest of the report out of the packet. Haynie appeared to have served an eight-month sentence for a drug-related charge. Not too long an incarceration, but any time inside normally had cons avoiding all law enforcement like the plague upon release. So why had he filed a report about stolen property when it didn't amount to a loss of more than a hundred or so bucks at most?

Gary checked the dates in the report. Haynie had been released eleven months ago. Had served a six-month probation period with no violations reported by his parole officer. Gary made a note to check with Jon Garrison, the new parole officer for Vermilion parish. Maybe he could get copies of the parole officer's personal notes.

It was possible Haynie had become overcautious since his release. It happened in a few instances, where cons became so accustomed to guards, wardens and parole officers that they ran to local lawmen over every little thing. Haynie sure fit the profile of that type of con. But his failure to mention his prison record was enough to raise Gary's suspicions.

Bob ambled into the office carrying a coffee cup. "I'll be glad to wrap up this case. My stomach can't take the food here much longer."

Gary glanced up and shook his head. "Why don't you try eating some of the seafood rather than burgers and fries?"

"Well, Mike said I should really try the double bacon cheeseburger."

Gary's stomach turned just thinking about the fat content. He dropped Haynie's report on Bob's temporary desk. "Got the goods on Haynie."

"Clean?"

"Nope."

"Really?" Bob set down the cup and snatched the folder. "Drugs? I'd never have guessed it."

"Actually, it fits him. Keep reading. He got a lighter sentence because he made a plea with the U.S. Attorney's Office, meaning he rolled on someone. He's a snitch."

"Explains why he's a *gypsy,* too."

"Right. In most drug cases, you turn over evidence on a dealer, distributor or manufacturer, and you're a dead man. He has to keep moving."

Bob shook his head. "Better keep looking over his shoulder."

"Yep." Something niggled against his subconscious. Something about Haynie, but what? "I think I'm gonna run back out to talk to Haynie again. Shake the trees and see what falls."

"Mind if I ask Mike to take me out to Fenton's place again? I still think there's some connection between father, son and Ms. Harris."

"Go for it." Gary informed Missy where he'd be and headed to the cruiser.

The afternoon sun heated the asphalt of the parking lot. Spring would arrive in Lagniappe before they realized it, wreaking havoc on Gary's allergies.

The drive to Haynie's place passed in a blur as Gary considered where he'd take Monique tonight. Cajun's Wharf had recently completed some renovations, trying to draw in a more upscale crowd. Maybe he should call and make reservations?

He pulled into the driveway and immediately noticed the absence of the sedan. Could Haynie be out looking for part-time work? Buying or selling something? Who knew? Gary knocked on the door. No response. He rapped a little harder. Still not a sound from inside.

Wouldn't hurt to look around again.

Moving to the backyard, Gary stared at the distance from the shed to the bayou. Possible escape route for the thief? No, not a chance Haynie wouldn't have heard the boat engine. No mistaking the noise for a coon. When Mike had come out and filed the report, he'd checked for tire tracks around the shed, but nothing had been detected. So the thief left on foot? Toting a battery charger, voltage meter and twenty-five gallons of fuel? Not hardly. Seemed more like Haynie was lying about the whole deal. But why?

Gary went back to his car, but he still couldn't figure out what kept bugging him. He started the car, his stomach rumbling. He'd better swing by his mom's for lunch. She'd left a couple of messages on his voice mail that he hadn't returned yet. He glanced at the clock. His mother would be home. Tuesdays and Thursdays were her days off from the diner.

He'd barely put the cruiser in Park when his mother came out of the house. "It's about time. I was ready to file a missing persons report."

He chuckled and kissed her proffered cheek. "Sorry, Mom. Been hectic."

"Working on Monique's case?"

"Yeah." He tossed an arm around her shoulders as they headed into the house. The aroma of fresh-baked bread filled the air. His stomach growled.

"How's it going?"

"You know I can't give you details." He slumped into a kitchen chair.

"I'm assuming you're hungry?" She didn't wait for an answer, just began preparing him a thick turkey sandwich made on homemade bread. "I like that girl. There's something about her that's special."

"I know." He spoke more to himself than his mother.

But she didn't miss a beat. She plopped the plate in front of him and took the opposite chair. "Son, do you have feelings for her?"

"I hate to admit it, but I do."

"Why would you hate to admit that? She's lovely."

He sent up a silent prayer, then took a sip of milk. "Because she isn't a Christian, Mom."

His mother shook her head. "Boy, that girl knows God just as surely as you and I do. I can tell these things."

He swallowed the bite of sandwich and took another drink. "She flat-out told me she wasn't on speaking terms with God."

Della laughed. "Son, you truly can be dense, can't you?"

"What?"

"We all get mad at God sometimes. That's natural. And I don't think it riles the good Lord up any, either."

"Yeah, but she's not talking to Him. That's different than being mad."

"You think?" His mother wiped crumbs into a paper napkin.

"Yes."

"I disagree with you there, son."

"In what way?"

"When you were a teenager and I wouldn't let you do something, you'd get angry with me, yes?"

"I suppose."

She chuckled. "Oh, you were mad all right. Trust me."

He snickered. "Okay, yes, I'd get mad at you. I remembered we'd argue till you'd order me to go to my room."

"That's because you drove me to the edge, boy." She chuckled and shook her head. "And then hours later, I'd call you out for supper. You'd come dragging up to the table and plop down. And what would you do?"

"Eat?" He finished off his sandwich and gulped down the rest of his milk.

"Yeah, you'd eat all right. But in silence. You wouldn't say a word to me."

"You'd sent me to my room."

"And you were mad and refused to talk to me."

"So?"

"Did you love me any less then?"

He pulled himself up. Had he? He'd been mad when she wouldn't let him do things his friends got to do. He'd felt left out, like his friends were making fun of him behind his back because his mommy wouldn't let him go. But he knew now it was because they couldn't afford for him to go to the movies or such. She hadn't done it to be mean.

"No."

She cackled. "Don't lie. At the time, did you love me less?"

"I don't know, Mom. Maybe. What's the point?"

"That you might have felt like you loved me less, but as you grew and matured and understood things, you didn't love me any less, right?"

"I loved you more."

She smiled and stood, patting his shoulder. "Exactly. But you wouldn't have understood all that back then."

"I still don't get your point."

Grabbing his plate and glass, she set them in the sink and then faced him. "Maybe Monique is at the end of the teenager phase in her spiritual life right now, where Father's calling her out to supper and she's being stubborn and not talking to Him. That doesn't mean she doesn't still love Him." She kissed his cheek. "Think about that for a while."

She wiped the table in front of him with a dish towel. "And think about maybe how you could help her see that sometimes understanding takes time. That's why they say hindsight is twenty-twenty. Monday morning quarterbacking is always easier than playing on Sunday night."

As usual, she was right.

Gary pushed to his feet and kissed her temple. "How'd I get so lucky to have such a wise mother?"

"Just blessed, I suppose." She laughed.

"I guess so. Thanks for everything, Mom."

Driving back to the station, he considered his mother's advice. *Dear God, guide me to be a living testament of You for Monique. Show me how to help her understand Your will.*

NINETEEN

What was she thinking?

Almost a decade had passed since Monique had been out on a date with anyone besides Kent. Why had she agreed to go out with Gary?

Because he was the first man since Kent who made her feel that maybe love could come her way again.

Standing in front of her closet, she stared at her meager options. Why hadn't she bought anything dressy when she'd gone clothes shopping with Felicia and CoCo? Since the fire, she'd only shopped for clothes once, and hadn't gotten anything that'd be considered remotely dressy.

She glanced at the two-year-old Catahoula she'd adopted this afternoon from the Humane Society. He sat staring at her with those incredible brown-and-blue puppy-dog eyes of his.

"Whatcha think, Homer?"

He tilted his head and made a throaty whine.

No help. She was crazy. Certifiable. She let out a sigh and grabbed her black tuxedo slacks and a white button-down shirt. They'd have to do. "Come on, Homer." She padded into the bathroom, the dog on her heels.

She'd barely finished applying her makeup and fighting with her hair, which refused to cooperate, when a knock sounded at the front door.

Homer ran down the hall, his toenails clicking against the wood floor.

Monique tossed the brush into the basket on the vanity, stuck her tongue out at her reflection and followed the dog. "Homer, quiet down. Sit. Good boy." She opened the door slowly, keeping the dog in her peripheral vision.

Gary stood in the doorway, dressed in a pair of khaki slacks and a blue sweater that brought out the clarity of his eyes. Her heart pounded against her throat. "You look lovely." He handed her a small bouquet of mixed flowers.

Oh, her heart really thumped now.

"Th-thank you." She opened the door all the way. "Come on in. I need to let Homer out before I leave."

Gary knelt in front of the dog, who continued to make intermittent throaty growls. "You really adopted one."

"Yep. He's a good watchdog, at least from what the lady at the Humane Society said." She noticed the cautiousness with which Homer sniffed Gary. "I think she's right."

"A Catahoula, huh?" Gary stroked the dog's head.

"Why not? Figured it was appropriate, since the breed began here in Louisiana."

"They're great treeing dogs."

"So I've been told." Monique smiled and raked her teeth over her bottom lip. "Come on, Homer. Outside." She moved to the kitchen and opened the door.

The dog ran around, sniffing around the bayou's edge.

"He's already a great companion. He laid at my feet while I sat in my rocker this afternoon reading." Heat infused her cheeks.

"I'm glad you like the chair."

The dog ran back up the steps. Monique shut the door behind him. She checked his bowls, refilled his water and then grabbed her purse. "Ready?"

Gary nodded and led the way out the front door. Homer stood in the doorway. Monique snapped her fingers. "Stay, Homer." The dog whimpered but dropped to his haunches.

She locked the door and pushed a button on her key fob. A beep sounded inside. "There, all set. I just hope Homer doesn't press too hard against the windows, or the alarm will go off."

"They got everything installed, yes?"

"All the bells and whistles, pun intended." She grinned as he led her to a truck. "Where's the cruiser?"

"I'm not on duty tonight. Is Luc coming back over to crash on your sofa again tonight?"

She smiled. "No. No curfew tonight. Since I got the alarm system and dog, I told him I'd be okay on my own."

Little zaps tingled through her as he placed his hand on the small of her back while he opened the passenger door. Tucked inside, she watched him walk in front of the truck to get behind the wheel. She couldn't help but notice the confidence in his walk, the strong lines of his posture....

He opened the door. "I took the liberty of making reservations at Cajun's Wharf. Hope that's okay?"

"I guess. I have no clue."

"Good. They serve really good food, but just finished some remodeling, so I'm anxious to see how it's changed."

On the ride to the restaurant, she told him about the meeting with Marshall Hudson. She finished as he pulled into the parking lot. "So, needless to say, I'm thinking that special fund should be deposited into the regular Trahan trust account."

"Sounds good to me." He shook his head and led her into the restaurant. "Ole Beau...he was devious, that's for sure. But from what I've heard, because of Justin's reputation, Beau would've had reason to think Justin would have heirs coming out of the woodwork."

The hostess seated them almost immediately. A corner window table—wow, he must really rate. A candle sat atop a mirror in the center of the table, creating a romantic setting. Soft classical music filtered in from the overhead speakers. And the aroma filling the restaurant...it made her mouth water just to sit and smell the spices.

Over bread and tea, they made small talk. She sensed that he wanted to talk to her about something specific but held back. "How was your day?"

"Not bad. I spent it working the case. I'd like to run a couple of names by you, just to see if you recognize them."

"Sure."

"Know a Niles Patterson or Kevin Haynie?"

She swallowed the bread. "No, should I?"

"Just some locals who popped up on the suspect list." He brought her up to speed on the interviews he'd conducted.

"I'm sorry. I wish I recognized either of them."

"Me, too."

The waitress appeared with their entrees of jambalaya, providing a welcome reprieve. The food was excellent, prepared with just the right amount of spice for flavor, but not enough to burn her throat.

For some reason, Monique didn't sense the ease she normally felt around Gary. Had she been out of the dating scene so long she couldn't relax and enjoy a date with a man she genuinely cared about? Her emotions were all tangled and twisted. Maybe she should've figured out what she really felt before she accepted his invitation.

But as she looked across the table into his eyes, she knew that, given the same opportunity, she'd accept his invitation all over again, without analysis.

Despite the discomfort and awkwardness.

He was blowing it big-time.

Gary struggled for something to say, when all he wanted to do was approach her about her relationship with God. Ever since his mother had talked with him, he'd been recharged and excited about discussing faith with Monique.

But now, sitting with her, he was afraid he'd upset her if he broached the subject. It wasn't like he could just blurt out, "Hey, you need to mature a little so you'll understand why God did whatever He did that made you so mad." Nope, wouldn't be the smartest way to introduce the subject.

He paid the check and they stepped out into the cool night. "Want to walk along the boardwalk for a little bit, or are you cold?"

"I'm fine. A walk sounds nice."

Taking her hand, he led her down the steps behind the restaurant to the boardwalk running alongside the bayou. Little battery-operated lights lined the walkway. The water lapped gently against the wood pylons, keeping time with their footfalls. The clean scents of earth and water surrounded them. A perfect scene, marred only by his own hesitation.

They walked a way before she stopped and turned to face him. "Would you just spit out what's on your mind? I can't stand the awkwardness anymore."

Gary looked into her animated green eyes, about to tell her how important her relationship with God was to him when something went awry. He carefully took her face in his hands. Her skin felt smooth and soft under his palms. Ducking his head, he put his lips to hers.

She responded, and his heart lurched. He pulled her into his arms, deepening the kiss. Strange things happened to him suddenly. His stomach tightened, his pulse raced and heat infused his spine. Like the flu or something.

He ended the kiss, fighting not to gasp for air, and stared into her clouded eyes.

She laid a hand against his cheek. The flu symptoms worsened. She ran her thumb over his bottom lip. Oh, he'd need an ER soon.

Tweedle. Tweedle. Tweedle.

She jumped back and opened her purse. "I can't imagine who'd call, except Felicia or Luc." She flipped open her cell and pressed it to her ear. "Hello."

Gary took the moment to regulate his breathing. He'd never felt this way, reacted this way to a woman before.

"Yes, this is she."

How had he gotten so sidetracked? Something about the way she looked at him…

"Yes. Code word is Justin, J-u-s-t-i-n."

He jerked his attention to her.

Her stare met his. "Hold on a moment." She pressed the mute button. "It's the alarm company. My alarm's been activated. The breakage sensor on the front window. It might just be Homer. They want to know if they should call the police."

"Tell them I'm with you and will check it out."

She pressed the button again. "I'm with a sheriff's deputy now. He said he'll take me home and check it out."

Gary silently prayed it was only the dog.

"Yes. Thank you." She closed the phone. "They said they'll call back in fifteen minutes for verification."

"Let's go." He led her up the steps and to the truck. After opening the door for her and letting her get settled, he opened the glove box and pulled out his service revolver.

Gary raced through town, wishing he'd brought the cruiser so he could use the lights and sirens. Cutting his eyes to her, he noticed her pallor. And the worry settling in her brow. "It's probably just the dog."

"I hope so. I don't know." She chewed her bottom lip.

He pressed the accelerator harder. Within minutes, he turned into her driveway. Lights flashed from her porch, as well as the motion sensor beams mounted on the four corners of the house. A wailing screech nearly burst his eardrums as they opened the doors.

Monique pressed the button on her key fob and silence settled over the bayou.

Gary withdrew his gun from its holster. "Stay here. I mean it." He crept alongside the house, eyes peeled for any type of movement. Rounding the corner to the back, he came upon Homer, barking furiously.

Gary ignored the dog and kept moving around the perimeter.

He stared intently at the bayou. Lots of places someone could hide. Although with the sirens and lights going off, if someone had been at the house, they were probably long gone now.

Unless they were just plain stupid.

He finished his walk-around and holstered his gun before returning to the truck, where Monique stood holding Homer's collar. "I didn't see anybody."

She sighed and pointed to the window. "Probably Homer. Looks like he broke it trying to get out." She moved toward the house.

He looked at the front window, studying the breakage pattern as he followed her. "Hold on, Monique."

She spun. "What?"

"I don't think the dog broke the window."

"Then what did?"

"I don't know. Let me check it out."

She unlocked the door, and he preceded her into the house. Homer nearly knocked him over, trying to nudge inside. "Down, boy. It's me."

Monique took hold of Homer's collar while Gary moved into the living room, hand on the butt of his firearm. Again, he didn't think anyone would be stupid enough to stick around after the alarm went off, but he'd rather be safe than sorry.

He flipped on the light in the living room. Everything looked the way it had when they'd left mere hours ago. But what did he know about little things out of place?

Then he saw it. Shards of glass littered the floor in front of the window.

A large rock with paper held securely by a rubber band lay in the middle of the glass.

Monique gasped behind him. "What's that?"

"A message, I'd guess." He secured the holster for his firearm. "Let me run out to my truck and grab some latex gloves. Go ahead and call your alarm company back and tell them what's going on. I'll call Mike and have him bring the crime scene kit over." He nodded at the dog. "You need to put him up some-where. I know he's probably already been all over the evidence in here, but we need to minimize contamination of the scene as much as possible."

As he headed out to the truck, he called Mike, all the while wishing he'd brought the cruiser. He explained to Mike what he needed, grabbed his spare latexes from the glove box and headed back inside. Although he was fairly certain no one was in the house, he didn't want to leave Monique alone.

He entered the house to find Monique walking down the hall, closing her cell phone. "Homer's shut in the bedroom, and the alarm company said they'd verify with your office." She shrugged. "I guess that's to make sure a deputy's really on-site?"

"Yeah, they do that." He popped the latex gloves on with a snap. "Do you have a digital camera?"

"I have all of Kent's." She turned, then froze. "No. All his equipment burned up in the fire." She trembled. "Why didn't I leave those in the truck with the guns?"

He pulled her into his arms and kissed her forehead. "Shh. It's okay."

She sniffled and leaned against him. He could so get used to this.

Sirens wailed, louder and louder. Strobing lights shone down the driveway.

Gary stepped away from her. "Mike's here with the kit."

She dabbed at the corners of her eyes and let out a sigh.

"You okay?"

"I'm fine. Thanks."

Mike stuck his head in the door. "In here?"

"Come on." Gary took the case from Mike and opened it. He passed the digital camera to the other man. "You know the drill. Whole living room, but focus on the window and the floor. Start with the floor so I can bag evidence. Then I need you to check the ground around the area outside. Try to find a footprint, track, anything."

"You got it, boss."

Gary stilled for a moment. Boss? He liked that. Shaking his head, he withdrew evidence bags from the kit. Mike finished snapping photos of the floor and moved on to the window. Gary slipped some of the glass into a bag, careful not to slice his gloves. He took the rock, carefully removing the rubber band and placing it in another bag.

He unwrapped the paper from the rock and smoothed it. Bold, black, block lettering stated the ominous message.

LAST WARNING: LEAVE.

TWENTY

Fury held her hostage.

Monique stared at the letter Gary held. To keep violating her things... The nerve of the creep.

Gary slipped the letter into an envelope. "We'll have the lab analyze this pronto. Fingerprints, paper, everything."

Monique didn't feel any better once the letter was tucked away. So what if it was out of sight? The letter had been yet one more thing to invade her peace. Her sense of belonging.

The other deputy moved outside, camera flash lighting constantly. When would the barrage end? When this jerk followed through with his threats? This one said it was her last warning. Would he come after her?

She had her guns, hadn't even gotten them out of the Expedition when she moved here, which was good, considering they'd have burnt up in the fire. She knew she could defend herself but the point was, she shouldn't have to. Counting the call to Hattie, this was his fifth contact. About five too many.

The deputy on the outside talked to Gary through the hole in the window. "I have some duct tape in the kit. If we tape it from both sides that should be good to hold it overnight."

"Good thinking." Gary dug in the kit and pulled out the silver tape. He secured several strips over the hole on the inside, then took the roll outside. He came back inside and bent to retrieve all the evidence bags.

"Maybe you should call Luc to come stay tonight."

"I have the alarm system and Homer. I'm fine." What could any of them do? Nothing. Not Gary, not the entire Vermilion parish sheriff's office. And she wouldn't call Luc and put him in danger. She could handle this on her own.

She *would* handle this herself.

Gary stood and placed the evidence bags in the case. "If you'll get me a broom, I'll clean up this glass for you."

"You know what you can do for me? Find this guy. Make him stop bothering me." Maybe she was misdirecting her anger, but seriously…five times he'd pushed her, and the police still hadn't apprehended him.

Gary's Adam's apple bobbed against the collar of his sweater. "We're doing everything we can, Monique."

"It's not enough. He's still able to get to me. My security system, my dog—they're all measures I've taken to protect myself. What has the sheriff's department done but come after the fact and clean up the mess? I've had enough."

"That's not fair. We have laws, rules that we have to foll—"

"You follow those rules but it doesn't get me anywhere, does it? You don't know who this guy is, where he is, why he's targeting me."

"We don't have much to go on. You know that."

"Yeah, but I also know I can't take much more of this." Her voice hitched on the last word, but she didn't care. She was tired of being violated. Tired of being threatened. Tired of getting no answers.

Gary stared at her, pain shimmering in his eyes.

No, she wouldn't let her attraction for him distract her. This guy had to be found and stopped. Before he finally came after her, instead of her property. She steeled her heart. "Are you finished here?"

"Monique."

"Are you done, *Deputy?*"

His jaw hardened as he glanced out the window. "I think so."

"Then I guess you should go. Get back to the office and file a report."

"Monique."

"Just go. Please." Her throat tightened, but she needed him to leave before she broke down. It was all too much for her right now. "And don't you dare call Luc or Spence. I don't need a babysitter. I can handle this just fine on my own."

"I'll call you in the morning." He took a step toward her, stopped for a moment, then turned and strode out the door.

She dead-bolted the lock and activated the alarm system. Leaning against the door, she inhaled slowly. Until he'd left, she wouldn't break down. She couldn't chance him coming back for something and seeing her crying.

After retrieving the broom and dustpan from the kitchen pantry, she cleaned up the glass. She'd have to call someone to replace the window in the morning. Would she forever be spending her days repairing or replacing what this creep took from her?

She made her way down the hall and opened the bedroom door. Homer nearly knocked her over. She stroked his head and moved back into the living room. The taillights from the cruiser and Gary's truck dimmed as they turned onto the road.

Sinking onto the couch, she released the pent-up tears. Her body shook as she sobbed. Homer jumped onto the cushion beside her, nudging her with his snout. She wrapped her arms around the bulk of a dog and cried into his fur.

What a mess her life had become. She'd once thought she had a charmed life. Ha. That was back when she'd just married Kent and they were building his business. So much had happened since then. So much change. Not that all of it was bad—finding her cousins was wonderful, but losing Kent had nearly killed her.

Now it seemed someone was determined to finish the task.

She sniffed and gave Homer's chin a good rub. She glanced around the room. Maybe she should be satisfied that she had a house, a family and a good dog. But her heart screamed out for more. It wanted love.

Gary's image drifted across her mind.

She'd been horrible to him. It wasn't his fault this jerk kept coming after her. "Oh, Homer, I'm such an emotional mess."

The dog tilted his head and stared at her. A moment later, he licked the end of her nose.

She laughed and hugged him again. Her gaze lit on Felicia and Spence's housewarming gift. Such a peaceful photograph. Without intent, she read the second part of the Scripture aloud. "You will protect me from trouble."

Really? Sure didn't feel like she was being protected. Kent hadn't been protected. Her mother hadn't been protected. Monique's entire life hadn't been protected. How could this Scripture make such a promise?

Curious and determined, she grabbed her purse from the buffet just inside the door. Homer looked at her like she was crazy and went to his food bowl in the kitchen. Monique's hand automatically wrapped around Kent's Bible in the side pocket of her purse. She went back to the couch and flipped through the pages until she found Psalm 32. She began reading at verse 1. She sucked in air when she got to verse 9.

Do not be like the horse or the mule, which have no understanding but must be controlled by bit and bridle or they will not come to you.

Had she become like a horse or mule? Too stubborn to go where she should?

Something in her heart jumped in response to her questions. Her eyes went back to the text.

Which have no understanding but must be controlled.

Was God trying to get her attention? Lead her into understanding? Had she resisted to the point where she had to be controlled?

Everything inside her seemed to hum.

New tears searing her eyelids, she dropped to her knees and prayed.

He didn't deserve the promotion.

Gary berated himself as he dragged himself into the office that night. Monique had been right—he hadn't been able to find the arsonist, much less catch him.

"I'll get the reports put into the system," Mike called as he moved down the hallway.

"When you're done, would you mind staking out Ms. Harris's house?" Gary asked.

Mike grinned and slightly ducked his head. "For some strange reason, I think it best if I did all the stakeouts. Didn't exactly sound like she was happy with you tonight."

"No, she wasn't." Gary ran a hand down his scrubbed face. "Thanks. I'll cover things here in the morning so you can get some sleep."

"No worries. I'm used to functioning on little to no sleep. Military does that to you."

Mike would actually be a great chief deputy. Attentive, smart and the guy had great cop instincts.

Gary shuddered as his dream took a nosedive. He shoved away the grief and focused on filling out the lab requests. Why couldn't he get a lead on this guy? There had to be something, some little clue he'd missed.

After finishing the lab forms, he pulled out his notebook. Maybe rereading his notes, fresh, would give him a new approach. Or at least a direction in which to go.

An hour into reading and Mike stuck his head in the door. "All done with the reports. Need me to do anything else before I head to Ms. Harris's place?"

"No. Thanks, Mike."

After the deputy left, Gary continued to reread his notes. Then the reports on Niles Patterson, Terrence Fenton and Kevin

Haynie. There was something here, he just knew it. Felt it. His vision blurred, and he rubbed his eyes. Why couldn't he find it? Frustration rammed against his skull.

Father God, I come to You in desperation. I know the link to the arsonist is here, but my human eyes are blinded. I pray for wisdom, for You to show me the light on which direction to take.

He'd better call it a night before he fell asleep at the desk. Shutting his notebook, he slipped it back into his pocket and then pushed the reports back into their folders. He checked to make sure he hadn't mixed up any papers when his gaze fell on the rap sheet of Kevin Haynie. His eyes went to the incarceration history.

Eight months incarcerated on petty drug charges. Released February of last year. Served six months parole, was released from parole in August.

Something…

He flipped through the pages to get to more detail. Finally, he found the presentence report, judge's orders and incarceration paperwork.

Sentenced to eight months at Oakdale Federal Correctional Institution in Louisiana.

The same prison Justin Trahan was serving time in!

Could be nothing—a druggie, murderer and arsonist didn't exactly make common bedfellows, but stranger things had happened. And it gave Haynie a connection to Monique.

Gary turned on his computer and waited for it to boot up. If he could find out if there was a relationship between Justin and Kevin, he'd have a lead. He struggled to keep his hopes from soaring.

After logging into the government system, he accessed the prison facility in Oakdale, then did an inmate search. While Oakdale had a satellite prison camp, which Haynie should've qualified for with his short sentence, he'd been put in low security, which was where Justin served. Gary recalled being shocked that a double murderer had been sentenced to a low-security prison, but Justin was a Trahan, and that meant money. Big bucks had a lot of pull, even on a federal level. And if Justin was somehow connected to these threats against Monique…

Gary pulled the warden's e-mail address, opened his mail program and shot off an e-mail requesting more information regarding Kevin Haynie and Justin Trahan. Too bad it was so late. But using his deputy sheriff's title and return e-mail, he should get an answer first thing tomorrow morning.

Might be nothing, but it was more than what he had to go on now.

Grrrr!

Monique rolled over and eyed Homer. The dog stood at the window facing the bayou, his hackles raised.

She jumped out of bed and wrapped herself in a robe. "What is it, boy?" she whispered.

Homer continued to bark, mixing in a deep growl from his chest.

Goose bumps prickled her skin. She slipped on her Crocs and tiptoed to the window. Hiding behind the curtains, she peeked through the pane.

A full moon bathed the bayou, glistening and shimmering as the wind gently caressed the Spanish moss draped over tree limbs. Soft ripples made their way over the water to the bayou's edge.

The dog barked louder, followed by a growl.

"Shh, Homer. Quiet."

The dog stopped barking but continued to move toward the window. She grabbed his collar and jerked him behind her.

Then she heard it—movement outside the house.

She rushed to her closet, and grabbed her lockbox. Her fingers went numb as she fumbled with the lock. Finally, it opened, and she pulled out her 9 mm. Monique slipped it from its holster and slid off the safety. "Stay," she ordered Homer before creeping down the hall to the kitchen door.

After disengaging the alarm system, she eased off the dead bolt, pushed the door open a crack and peeked out. Nothing. She stole outside to the steps, nudging the door closed behind her. She stopped and listened, adrenaline pushing her ears into supersensitivity.

Footsteps came around from the back of the house.

She crept down the steps, avoiding the one that creaked, with gun held in ready position. The January air cooled the sweat lining her palms. She flexed her fingers and readjusted her hold on the gun's grip.

Slowly, she worked her back to the side of the house. Dew on the hedges smeared against her robe, chilling her. Her heart thudded in double time as she crept along the house.

The footfalls drew closer…closer…closer—

She pivoted and took a shooting stance, arms extended with left hand supporting the right holding the gun. "Freeze. I'm armed."

"Whoa, don't shoot!" The man thrust his hands to the heavens.

"Who are you and what are you doing sneaking around my house? Keep your hands up where I can see them."

"I'm Mike, the deputy?" He took two steps toward her, into the half-light.

The badge on his chest shone in the moonlight. "See? It's me."

She lowered the gun and slipped the safety back in place. "What are you doing sneaking around my house?"

He ducked his head. "Checking things out."

She should've been angry, probably would have been had she not had a long, resolving talk with God prior to falling into bed. Now, she was touched. "Did Deputy Anderson put you up to this?"

"It's part of our job."

She smiled in the grayness. "I see. Well, I'm fine. You scared me silly, though."

"I'm sorry. I didn't know you had a dog that would alert you."

Right. Homer had been shut in her bedroom when Mike had come to help Gary with the crime scene. "It's okay. We're fine."

"Uh, you won't call Deputy Anderson and chew him out because you caught me checking things out, will you?"

She laughed. "No. I won't say anything."

"*Merci.* I really appreciate it."

"No problem. I'm going back in and going to bed now. Busy day tomorrow."

"Okay. Sorry for scaring you. I'll be out in my cruiser if you need anything."

"You don't have to stay all night. I have the dog, and we're fine."

"It's my post, ma'am."

And he couldn't abandon his post. "Good night, then."

"Night, ma'am."

After reassuring Homer that all was okay, Monique climbed back into bed with a yawn. Tomorrow, she'd have to find Gary and apologize for coming down so hard on him. He really was doing the best he could on the case. Wasn't his fault the creep didn't leave any clues behind.

She turned on her side and punched her pillow. It was nice of Gary to send Mike to keep watch over the house. He didn't have to, especially after the way she'd behaved, but he had. Because he cared.

Good thing, because she realized she had begun to care entirely too much for him, and writing him out of her life would rip her heart apart.

Her eyes popped open and she sat upright. She considered how she felt about Gary. The little things he did for her. How she felt when he was near her. The acceptance between them. The way his eyes made her stomach knot. How her heart did gymnastics when he smiled at her.

Oh, my. She was falling for Deputy Gary Anderson.

Falling hard.

TWENTY-ONE

Something cold against her back brought Monique out of a deep and restless slumber. She jumped and twisted in the bed. Homer nudged her with his cold nose. She smiled and rubbed behind his ears. "You need to go out, boy?" She stood and grabbed her robe. The terry cloth was still damp from last night. "Come on, I'll let you out and make some coffee."

As she padded to the kitchen, it occurred to her that she was talking aloud to a dog. Man, she'd better watch herself or she'd start collecting cats, as well.

After letting the dog out and putting the coffee on, she took a quick shower and dressed in jeans and a sweater. She let Homer back inside, filled his food and water bowls, then glanced out the front window while she enjoyed her first cup of joe.

No sign of the deputy or his cruiser. Daylight must have ended his watch. Her lips curved into a smile around the cup's rim. Would Gary take the post tonight?

Just thinking of him made her regret her words and manner toward him all over again. Especially now that she realized the depth of her feelings toward him. Now that she considered it, her unexplainable attitude could have contributed to those feelings. Mixed with confusion and uncertainty, of course.

Using the phone book, she found the number for a window company. Within minutes of making the call, they assured her they'd be out within an hour.

She walked through the living room, stopping to stare at the picture over the mantel. She smiled and offered up a morning prayer of thanksgiving and gratitude.

Brring!

She rushed to the kitchen to grab the phone, and answered breathlessly. "Hello?"

"What were you doing? Running a marathon, *Boo?*"

Monique grinned at CoCo's humor. "Don't I wish? How're you this morning?"

"Doing well. Listen, the reason I'm calling, aside from saying hello, is because I've asked Felicia and Spence to join Luc and me for *déjeuner* here at the house, and I'd love for you to come."

"Sounds like fun. What time?"

"Ten-ish. Will that work for you?"

"Sure."

"Great, we'll see you then."

"Uh, CoCo?"

"Oui?"

"I don't know where your house is."

CoCo chuckled and gave directions, then ended the call. Monique kept her hand on the phone. She knew she needed to call and apologize to Gary, but didn't know what else to say. How could she explain her mood swings without telling him how she felt? She didn't know if their relationship was something he wanted to pursue. She certainly couldn't blame him for writing her off after her deplorable behavior last night.

Her heart felt as if it would split. She wandered into the living room again, this time carrying the cordless phone, and sank onto the couch. She stared up at the picture again and then shook her head. It'd been a long time since she'd gone to the Bible for direction—it'd take a conscious effort to return to the habit.

She reached for Kent's Bible on the coffee table, held it lovingly in her hands, and prayed for God's guidance to the Scripture that would speak into her soul. Lifting her head, she flipped through pages, scanning, until she stopped in the book of Ephesians. Reading from the fourth chapter, verses 2 and 3, she found wisdom.

> *Be completely humble and gentle; be patient, bearing with one another in love. Make every effort to keep the unity of the Spirit through the bond of peace.*

She needed to make every effort to keep the unity of the Spirit through the bond of peace. Which meant she needed to call Gary, even though she knew it'd be difficult on her. She dialed the deputy's cell phone number and waited for two rings.

He answered on the third. "Anderson."

"Hi. It's Monique."

Gary's hand tightened around his cell. "Hi."

He could make out Monique's harsh breathing over the connection. "I need to apologize to you. I was extremely rude last night and there was no call for the way I acted."

"You were stressed, I understand that."

"No, there's more to it than that, but whatever the reason, I shouldn't have said such things to you, or kicked you out. I'm truly sorry."

"It's okay. I understand."

"I don't want things to be awkward between us now, ya know?"

"Yeah." He didn't want that either, but he wondered if there would ever be an *us* in regard to the two of them.

"I had an interesting conversation last night." Hesitation filled her tone.

"With whom?"

"God."

His heart lurched. "Oh?"

"Yeah. I've been stupid and ornery."

He couldn't help it; he chuckled.

She laughed, as well. "You don't have to agree so easily, ya know."

"I'm glad, Monique. Really glad."

"Me, too."

Should he say anything about his e-mail to the prison in Oakdale? He didn't want to upset her just yet. There still wasn't any proof that the attacks against her had anything to do with her father. He hadn't heard back from the warden this morning, which annoyed him. The Bureau of Prisons, it appeared, didn't adhere to the same code of responding quickly to law enforcement requests as other branches under the Department of Justice.

"And I did have a wonderful time on our date."

He yanked himself out of his reprieve, not believing she broached the subject he thought she'd avoid. "I did, too."

"I'm sorry I ruined it."

"You didn't. You're the victim. The jerk doing this is the only one who ruined anything."

"Well, I wanted to apologize, and to thank you."

"Are you okay?"

"I'm fine. I'm fixin' to head over to Luc and CoCo's for brunch."

He grinned at her phrasing—already she sounded like she belonged in Lagniappe. That thought alone sent pinpricks of happiness all over him, but he didn't want to get sidetracked into thinking about how much she meant to him. Not right now. Not until he'd solved her case and put the arsonist away…made sure she was safe again. After that, well, he'd have to figure out what to do, but it'd take a lot of time in prayer.

"Well, have fun. Tell them both I said hello."

"Will do."

He closed his cell phone and stared at the computer screen. No time to analyze his love life, or complications thereof. He had a case to crack. He dialed the number for the Oakdale Prison, gave his credentials, asked for the warden and was put on hold. Not even elevator music came behind the distinctive click.

Bob shuffled into the office doorway. Gary waved him in just as a voice came over the phone.

"Warden Prikton. How may I help you, Deputy Anderson?"

"I need some information on a con released from your facility on February third of last year."

"Inmate's name?"

"Kevin Haynie."

Bob's bushy eyebrows shot up. Gary grinned and nodded.

"What specifically are you looking for, Deputy?"

"I need to know if he was a cell mate, or in close contact either through the work programs or guard observations, with an inmate still in your facility. Justin Trahan."

Bob's eyes widened so much Gary thought the man's eyeballs might pop out. Gary grinned again. Yeah, it was an *aha* moment.

"Let me check. I'm looking to see if they were cell mates. As far as guard observations go, that'll take me some time."

"Warden, this is of the utmost importance to an open case I'm working. As fast as you could get the information to me, I'd greatly appreciate it."

"Well, they weren't cell mates, according to the computer records, but they were in the same unit. I'll check with the guards on duty now. I'll call you back after I've spoken with them."

"I really appreciate it." Gary rattled off the station and his cell phone numbers, then hung up.

"Haynie and Trahan? That's an odd combo."

"But it's a viable connection."

"So far."

"Yeah, but considering we don't have much else, I'm going with that."

Bob grunted. "Seems a lot of leads are comin' out of the woodwork real quick here."

"I need to focus on motive for each of them. If the attacks are related to her husband's murder case, motive would be to shut her up." He rubbed his chin. Whiskers met his touch. He'd forgotten to shave this morning.

"Don't stress too much about in-depth motive here, Anderson."

"Why?" Police procedural rule one: always start with motive.

"This arsonist, he loves his work. Loves the fire. Is entranced by fire." Bob leaned the wooden chair back on two legs. "Wouldn't be surprised if he'd started many other fires and never gotten caught. These kinds of freaks don't need a whole lot of motive to do what they do."

Gary let that information stew for a minute. "But the threats, the calls…that would indicate a deep motive."

"True." Bob dropped all four legs of the chair to the floor and sat straight. "Unless the arsonist isn't the one making the threats."

"It has to be the same person. It all fits."

"Unless your arsonist is a freelancer for hire. Then, heaven help us tie it all together."

"Glad you could make it." CoCo hugged her tight. "Come on in, we're all in the kitchen."

Monique followed her hostess through the walkway. "You have a beautiful home."

"Thanks. When Luc and I married, we both lived in family homes, which family still needed to live in. We'd found some Confederate coins in my house, and we sold those coins to Confederate museums for the money to build this place." CoCo chuckled. "It's a long story, one I'll have to tell you another time, but we love that it's right on the bayou so I can still do my job, and it's almost exactly between his old home and mine."

"Well, I can't wait to hear the story, but your home is wonderful."

"Hey." Felicia stood to hug Monique, followed by Luc and Spence.

CoCo waved Monique to the chair beside Felicia. "Sit down, sit down." She almost bubbled with energy. Her smile brought out the true exotic beauty of her Cajun heritage. For a second, Monique wished her hair were any color but the bland auburn she'd inherited from her mother.

"Luc and I have something very important to tell y'all. We wanted you to share in our joy."

"You're pregnant, yes?" Felicia all but jumped in her seat.

"Yes! I found out while I was in N'Awlins."

Felicia rushed around the table to hug her brother and sister-in-law. "Oh, congratulations. I'm going to be an aunt."

Spence clapped Luc's shoulder. "Congratulations, man."

Monique smiled, but couldn't help have a fleeting thought of her and Kent's plans to have a family. As quickly as the thought came, it left. With no pain left aching in her heart. Her smile widened. "Congratulations. When are you due?"

"Early September." Luc's eyes shimmered. "We're so excited."

"Have you told Alyssa and Tara?" Felicia asked.

"They were there when I found out. I got sick and Alyssa's doctor told me I should run a test."

"Oh, how perfect."

"And Grandmere's beside herself."

Felicia froze and stared at her brother. "Mom's not here. Are you not telling her?"

Luc laughed. "We went by yesterday and told Mom. Figured she'd throw a fit if she found out the same time as everyone else."

Felicia giggled. "Bet she's already ticked that Alyssa and Tara knew first."

"Yeah, but we let her know she was in the loop before you." Luc gently tugged his sister's hair.

"I don't care, I'm just so happy."

Monique reveled in the love of her family. She sent up a silent prayer of thanks that God had delivered her to these wonderful people. She looked around the table, amazed at the blessings surrounding her.

God was so good, even when she didn't realize it.

TWENTY-TWO

"Deputy Anderson." Missy's voice burst through the intercom. "A Warden Prikton is on line one for you."

Gary snatched up the receiver. "Deputy Anderson."

"This is Warden Prikton. I've got some information for you on the relationship between Haynie and Trahan."

Gripping his pen tighter, Gary nudged his notebook in front of him. "Go ahead." He poised the pen over the paper.

"None of the guards I spoke with recall anything between Haynie and Trahan. Of course, some of them aren't on duty today."

Gary's heart plummeted to his toes.

"But on instinct, I checked Trahan's visitor's log. Wasn't too long of a list to wade through, to tell you the truth."

"And?" Get to the point, man!

"Over the last two-plus years of incarceration, Trahan's only had three visitors besides his lawyer. His great-niece, Felicia Bertrand, a Monique Harris and two visits by none other than Kevin Haynie."

"Wait a minute—I didn't think cons could come back and visit inmates."

Prikton let out a heavy sigh over the line. "It's not common for it to happen, but once they're off parole, it's hard to keep track of them. According to the records I found this morning, the counselor who approved Haynie on Trahan's visitors' list was discharged a couple of months ago."

"You couldn't find him to ask?"

"Deputy, this is off the record, but we fired him for selling contraband to inmates. It happens in the best prisons."

Now it made sense. "When did Haynie visit Trahan?"

"Let's see, Haynie was released last February. He visited Trahan once on October tenth of last year, and again on December twelfth."

"How long were the visits?"

"According to the visitor's log, the one in October lasted three hours and ten minutes. The one in December lasted an hour and forty-five minutes."

A sick feeling turned in Gary's gut. "That's it?"

"Well, I spoke with one of the trustees who works in the mail room about the correspondence for Trahan."

"And?"

"He says Trahan and Haynie send letters back and forth. He remembered because that's the only general mail Trahan gets."

"Did he remember anything that was said in the letters?"

"I asked him. He just said there weren't any of the trigger words they look out for to return a letter."

"So we have no way of knowing what they could've been plotting?"

"I guess not."

"I really appreciate your thoroughness and getting back with me so quickly, Warden." Gary clicked his pen.

"There's one more thing you might want to know, Deputy."

"What's that?"

"Since the Second Chance Act has passed, lots of lawyers have been filing pleas and motions and such to get their older clients out of jail on the early release program. Especially ones with medical conditions."

Gary held his breath.

"Trahan's lawyer's one of 'em. According to my notes, Trahan has developed a heart condition and his medical report has been submitted to the committee for consideration of early release to a halfway house under the Second Chance Act."

Now Gary thought he'd be ill. "You're telling me Trahan's lawyer is trying to get him out early? Surely there's not a chance of that happening?"

"That's exactly what I'm telling you. And that could happen, because of this act."

Justin Trahan—double murderer—released into a halfway house? Would the Trahan name and money ever know limits?

Money... Justin's trust fund! That explained everything, or at least it could. Now to just find some proof!

"Did you miss me today, boy?" Monique scratched behind Homer's ears as he rested his head in her lap. She'd spent the better part of the day with Felicia and CoCo, brainstorming ideas for the baby's nursery. Though thrilled to be included, she was now exhausted. Sitting in the rocker Gary had given her, she glanced out over the bayou and rested her head against the back of the chair.

Just as she closed her eyes to doze for a few minutes in the afternoon peace, the shrill of the telephone brought her to her feet. She grabbed the cordless from the bedside table and slunk back into the rocker. "Hello?"

"You're a hard woman to find, Mrs. Harris."

The vaguely familiar voice caught in her mind, which was filled with sleep-induced cobwebs. "Who is this?"

He laughed. "Did I wake you? I'm sorry. This is Investigator Walkin in Monroe. The one who handled your husband's case?"

Sleep sped from every recess of her mind. She bolted upright. "Yes. I remember."

"I had the hardest time finding you. Good thing you have a listed number, and that deputy in Lagniappe called me. Otherwise, I wouldn't have found you so quickly."

She swallowed the sigh. Her new number was supposed to be unlisted. She'd have to call the phone company. "How can I help you?"

"I wanted to let you know that George Knight has been diagnosed with cancer in prison."

Her heart skipped a beat. The man who shot and killed Kent…cancer? "He's rather young, isn't he?"

"Forty-one, so, yeah. And it's stage four already. Took them a while to diagnose it."

In a prison, she could imagine the medical diagnostics and care would be less than ideal. "Oh."

What else was she supposed to say? She didn't even know what she felt right now.

"The reason I'm calling is because Mr. Knight requested a meeting with me. Said he had more information about your husband's case."

She just bet there was. "And?"

"Well, it seems you were correct. There was someone else involved in your husband's murder."

She knew it. Always had. "A driver?"

"Yes. Mr. Knight claims his cousin, Stanton Ogburn, was the driver of the car."

"The name doesn't ring any bells. Should it?"

"No. As far as we can tell, Mr. Ogburn had no connection to your husband."

"He lied to protect his cousin?"

"So it seems."

Frustration held her heart in a vise grip. "So, George Knight still claims the shooting was purely random?"

"Actually, he's recanted that. Since he's dying, he says he's found God and wants to tell the truth."

Hope sparked. "Really?"

"He now states that he and his cousin were hired to kill your husband and make it look like a drive-by shooting."

The air she sucked in turned to lead in her lungs. Her heartbeat thudded in her head, momentarily deafening her. "Who? Why?"

"Hold on, Mrs. Harris, this is all a dying man's statement. It's not fact yet."

"Why would he, if he's dying as you say, make up such a story?"

"To implicate his cousin. Maybe Ogburn wasn't even there but Knight's developed a grudge against him since he's been in jail. Who knows?"

But she knew. "I always said someone else was involved."

"And we'll keep looking into that angle."

"Who did George Knight say hired them to murder Kent? Why?"

"He said his cousin was the contact person. Took the money and set up the hit. Knight said he was only cut in on the deal to pull the trigger."

"So you don't have a clue who hired them or why?"

"Not yet. We've got an APB out on Ogburn right now. He wasn't at the last known address Knight gave us."

"But you *are* following up, right?" Oh, please. Don't let them drop the ball again. Not when she was so close to the truth. Finally, maybe she could put Kent to rest once and for all.

And move forward with her life.

A life that may include a very handsome and sensitive deputy sheriff.

"Of course. I'll let you know if we uncover anything." He paused. "There's more. From what Knight says, you were supposed to be in the car with your husband."

Her stomach tightened. Yes, she'd been working in the office with Kent at that time. But for someone to put a contract out on both of them? Why? She swallowed. "Thank you for telling me."

"And I'd appreciate it if you could tell that deputy friend of yours, too. He seems to be quite interested. Even called my supervisor to follow up."

"Sure." Gary had done all that without telling her? No wonder Walkin was calling her, basically asking her to call off the dogs.

"I appreciate that. Well, that's all I needed to tell you," Walkin said.

"Thank you for calling."

* * *

"That woman of yours packs a nine mil, did you know?"

Gary glanced up from his paperwork and narrowed his eyes. "I don't have a woman."

"Yeah. Okay." Mike chuckled and slumped against the office's door frame. "Either way, Monique Harris packs a nine mil, and isn't afraid to use it."

Oh, no. What had she done? "What happened?"

"Last night, I was walking along the back of her property, making sure no one snuck up from the bayou. Guess I made too much noise because out she came, in a fluffy blue bathrobe, and held me at gunpoint until she knew who I was."

Man. The woman had guts, he had to give her that. He smiled at the mental image of the little woman with copper curls, holding Mike at gunpoint in her robe.

"Sure, laugh." Mike chuckled along. "I'm sure it was quite a funny scene. But, just thought I'd let you know."

"She didn't even mention it when I talked to her earlier."

"I asked her not to call and ream you out."

Now it was Gary's turn to laugh. "Thanks, man. Appreciate that."

"No worries. So, I'll be out there again tonight."

"Thanks, Mike."

The deputy grinned and ambled down the hallway.

Gary looked back over his notes from the warden. Now that he had a link, he needed to let Monique know. He glanced at the clock—four. More than likely, she'd be out and about. The woman never seemed to stand still. He lifted the phone and dialed her cell number.

"Answer, Monique."

Gary listened to the third ring of her cell phone. Where was she?

The fourth ring sounded, then her voice mail clicked on. Where could she be? He left a brief message before hanging up.

Maybe she was one of those women who left their phones in

their vehicles when they got home. His mother did, probably because she was too unaccustomed to having a cell phone. She put it in the car's console and never even thought about it unless it rang while she was in the car. Good thing he'd told her to always leave it plugged in to the car charger—otherwise, her battery would forever be drained.

He dialed Monique's home number and waited. But not for long—she answered before the second ring could sound.

"Hello."

His heart jutted just at her voice. He so needed to get his feelings in line. When he had time. Right now he had to focus on the job and only that.

"Hey, Monique. It's Gary."

"I'm so glad you called. I just got off the phone with Investigator Walkin."

While he wanted to launch into what he'd learned, he could detect the excitement in her voice and felt honored she wanted to share her news with him. "What'd he say?"

She told him how Walkin had met with her husband's murderer, and discovered she'd been right all along—there *had* been someone else involved. But it was only a family member, which is why the triggerman took the fall—to protect his cousin. Gary's ears perked up as she told him that the man now stated they had singled out her husband because they'd been hired to do so, and make it look like a random drive-by. She told him that the murderer stated she was supposed to be included in the shooting.

His grip on the phone tightened. A hit ordered on both of them? Maybe she'd been right all along, and it did have something to do with Kent being a private investigator. "Have you looked through your husband's old files, found what he could've been working on that might've given someone a reason to hire someone to kill him?"

"I can't. My house burned down, remember?"

Guilt slammed against his chest. "I'm sorry."

She laughed, sounding almost carefree. "Don't be. It's a fact. But it's really nice to know I wasn't loony in what I believed."

"Well, I found out something interesting today, as well."

"Oh, me, too. Other than the news about the shooter, I mean."

He paused. Had she found out about her father and Haynie already? How? "What?"

"Well…I'm going to be a cousin again." Her voice lifted at the end.

"Huh?" She'd so lost him.

She giggled, actually giggled. The sound warmed him more than the air gusting from the heater's vent over the desk. "CoCo and Luc are expecting."

"Oh. Wow." He kept trying to envision CoCo pregnant. He couldn't picture her out in her airboat, tracking gators with a bulge in her belly. "That's great."

With Alyssa having just had a baby, and now with CoCo expecting, he couldn't help but wonder how long it would be before the sheriff announced that he and Tara were starting their family.

"I know. I spent the day with Felicia and CoCo, nursery planning."

He chuckled. "Poor Luc."

She giggled again. "So, what'd you find out?"

"About your case…"

"What?" All traces of laughter died from her voice.

He proceeded to tell her what the warden had told him.

A long pause hung over the connection when he'd finished.

"So, you think there's a connection between the arsonist and my biological father?"

"It's possible."

"That's so…I don't know, personal. I've barely even met my father, and I don't know this Kevin Haynie character at all. Why would he burn down my house?"

"I'm not saying he did. Remember, the gas was supposedly stolen from his place before your fire."

"But now that you've learned of his contact with Justin, you think it might be him?"

"It could be. I won't know anything until I find out more."

"I still don't understand."

How could he lay it out on the table without dragging up pain for her? "There's a good chance Justin's behind all of these attacks against you."

"Why?"

"For the trust-fund money."

"But why just warn me to leave? Why not just kill me?"

"Maybe because whomever Justin hired isn't very successful."

She sighed. "I suppose."

"There's more."

"What?"

Oh, this was what he dreaded telling her. "The warden said that Justin's lawyer has been filing paperwork to get him an early release due to a medical condition and the passing of some new act."

"What?"

He told her all the details he knew, then waited in silence.

"I can't believe they'd even hear an argument to let him out early. A halfway house? For a double murderer? Are they insane?"

"If you'd like, I can find out when the hearing is scheduled to take place. You're entitled to attend."

"Please do. I'm sure Felicia and Luc would like to know, as well."

"I'll let you know." Just as soon as he figured out a way to get the proof he needed. His top priority was to keep Monique safe, independent streak of hers or not.

That new dog of hers began barking in the background. "Hey, your mom just pulled up. Looks like she's got a big dish for me."

"Probably a casserole." He loved his mother, but sometimes, her timing messed with his social life.

She laughed. "Good. I haven't finished stocking up on staples yet and wondered what I would eat for supper. A PB and J was sounding mighty good." Her voice became muffled. "Down, Homer. Sit. Stay." She got louder. "She's at the door. Thanks for filling me in. Let me know when you find out the date." And she hung up before he could tell her goodbye, much less ask her out.

Oh, yeah. His mother's timing really left a lot to be desired.

TWENTY-THREE

The phone rang on Gary's bedside table, startling him. He must've dozed off. He scrubbed a hand over his face and lifted the receiver. It'd better be important. "Anderson."

"This is Investigator Walkin, from Monroe?"

Gary sat up straight and glanced at the clock—ten. "Yes, I remember." Why was the man calling him? How'd he gotten Gary's home number?

"I don't know if Mrs. Harris informed you of recent information regarding her husband's case or not—"

"Yes, she told me today."

"Good. Well, we were able to apprehend Stanton Ogburn, Knight's cousin."

"The driver?"

"Yes. After leaning on him and informing him that Knight had rolled on him, we learned who hired them to take out her husband." The man let out a heavy breath. "I would've called Mrs. Harris herself, but due to the late hour, I thought I'd better call you instead. Especially since you called and inquired. I had to pull rank on your dispatcher to get your number."

"Of course."

"Ogburn confessed to being the driver and setting up the shooting, and at this point, with the evidence provided, I have no reason to doubt his statement."

Get on with it. "Right."

"He says a fellow inmate from prison, Justin Trahan, hired them to do the deed after Ogburn was released. I checked with the warden at Oakdale and he verified Ogburn and Trahan were cell mates. He also told me you'd asked about Trahan, as well, so I figured I'd give you a call."

Bingo! Everything went straight back to Justin.

"Thanks, Investigator. I really appreciate your call."

"Figured it's the least I could do. Mrs. Harris swore up and down Knight hadn't acted alone and her husband's murder wasn't random. Guess she was right all along."

He got off the phone, his mind racing. Justin Trahan had paid to have Monique's husband killed? He'd probably paid to have Haynie burn down her house and threaten her, too. But why?

Gary lifted the phone and dialed her number. They were too close to finding out the truth. Justin had murdered his nephew and his brother, and tried to murder his great-nephew. He'd hired someone to kill Monique's husband.

He wouldn't think twice about having Monique murdered, as well.

Grrr!

Monique looked up from her book. "Homer, quiet." She glanced out the window across the bayou, studying the landscape. Nothing seemed amiss. Probably Deputy Mike out making his nightly rounds. She smiled to herself and took note of the time—10:15 p.m. Where had the time gone? She must've really gotten involved in the book she'd been reading.

She stood and stretched. Homer whimpered. She rubbed his head. "No, boy, we're not going out there tonight. It's bedtime." She snapped and pointed to the canine pillow at the foot of her bed.

The dog whimpered again, then plopped onto the pillow. Monique chuckled and got ready for bed. Her head barely hit the pillow before her eyelids collapsed.

* * *

No answer! Where was she? Too late to be out.

Gary dialed Monique's cell phone. Four rings and voice mail picked up.

Something wasn't right.

Pulling on jeans and a tee, he raced to the living room and lifted the mic from the radio unit he kept at home. He called into the dispatcher, asking to be patched through to Mike's unit. Gary slipped his feet in boots while he waited for the patch to go through.

"Deputy Anderson, no response from that unit."

For once, he really wished Missy was on duty. She'd try until Mike answered her. "Try again, please."

"Hold on," she said and sighed loudly.

First thing in the morning, he'd deal with the nighttime dispatcher's attitude and lack of initiative. Right now, he could only focus on Monique.

"Still no answer, Deputy Anderson."

Frustration nearly choked him. "Thank you."

He reached for his cell, punching in the speed-dial number for Mike. It went straight to voice mail. What was it with people not having their phones on them or turned off?

All sorts of scenarios played out in his mind... Mike didn't answer the radio because he'd seen someone snooping around Monique's place and had gotten out of his vehicle in a hurry. He left his cell in there, as well.

Didn't work with the phone being off, which the call going directly to voice mail usually indicated.

Okay, Mike took his cell, but is creeping up on the guy and doesn't want to blow the element of surprise, so he turned off the phone.

That made sense. It was logical.

Gary grabbed his service weapon and keys, running to the cruiser.

But it also meant someone was on Monique's property.

Wwrrp! Wwrrp!

Monique bolted upright in bed. What in blue blazes was that sound?

Homer jumped up on the bed, whining and putting his paws over his ears.

She threw off the covers and grabbed the dog's collar, then raced to the alarm keypad in her bedroom.

The code for the smoke alarm flashed.

Her heart nosedived. Not again.

Homer whined.

"Sorry, boy. I can't deactivate the alarm or the fire department might not come." She sniffed as she pulled on jeans and a tee—she couldn't smell any smoke. She grabbed her gun and slipped it in her waistband against her back.

She pulled out Homer's leash and clicked it onto the ring on his collar. "Come on, boy. Let's get out of here." She headed down the hallway to the front door, only to find it was stuck. Her heart caught in her throat.

Wait a minute—she couldn't smell any smoke, she couldn't see any flames and she didn't hear any crackling.

Monique peeked out the front window. The cruiser sat on the road at the end of the driveway. Surely Deputy Mike had heard her alarm and would come to check?

Spinning, she tugged Homer's leash and headed to the kitchen door. She gripped the knob and turned. Nothing. She pushed against the wood. The door didn't budge.

Her heart thudded. She was trapped, and her house was on fire!

She ran back to her bedroom, dragging the dog behind her. She tried to open the window to no avail. With both hands, she lifted the rocker Gary had given her and hurled it through the window. Glass shot to the ground, and the rocker cleared the small cobblestones past the hedges.

A loud boom rattled the house, and smoke filled the room. It must've needed oxygen to spread. And spreading it was. Already, she could hear the telltale crackling as the flames ate their way down the hall.

Monique grabbed a pillow from the bed and laid it over the sill. She eased herself out, then gently tugged on the leash, coaxing Homer to jump. He resisted.

Another loud boom rocked the house. Homer jumped, nearly knocking her down. "Good boy." Letting go of the leash, she ran down the driveway, toward the cruiser.

Sirens wailed somewhere off the main road.

She panted as she reached the police car. Bending, she peered inside to find Deputy Mike slumped over the seat. A cell phone battery lay on the seat beside him. The radio sat silent.

Homer barked and growled in the distance behind her.

She spun.

Something went over her face. She couldn't breathe. With flailing hands she reached for what was over her head.

A sharp pain split the back of her head. White dots danced before her eyes. A brief moment of nausea washed over her.

And everything went dark.

TWENTY-FOUR

Gary's chest tightened until he thought he could no longer breathe.

Fire trucks led the way to Monique's house. He flipped on his lights and siren, as well, racing behind the fire department's engine. They turned onto Wyatt Lane. Smoke filled the bayou.

Déjà vu all over again.

He skidded to a stop beside Mike's cruiser and jumped out of the car. Mike lay slumped back against the headrest. Gary's hand shook slightly as he checked the other deputy's pulse. Slow, but strong and steady. Not wanting to disturb any evidence, Gary went back to his cruiser and radioed in to the dispatcher, then changed radio frequencies and radioed to the EMT unit at the burning house to order attention for his deputy.

Torn between staying with Mike or rushing to the house to check on Monique, Gary bowed his head.

Father God, I can't be in two places at once, so I pray You keep everyone safe and show me where You want me to be.

Another EMT unit shuddered to a halt beside him. "Got the call a deputy needed medical assistance." The paramedics jumped out of the truck and grabbed cases.

Gary nodded toward Mike. "His pulse is slow, but strong."

"We got it. You go on up to the house and see what you can do there," the driver of the unit said.

That was all the sign Gary needed.

He hopped into his car and sped down the gravel driveway. Rocks pinged against the cruiser's undercarriage. He continued to pray silently for Monique's safety. He jammed the car into Park and rushed from the vehicle. Homer ran up to him, barking furiously.

"Where is she, boy? Huh? Where is she?" He grabbed the dog's collar and headed toward the fire trucks.

"Have you found anyone inside?" he asked.

Daniel, a member of his church, turned and faced him. "No one's inside. We think we've got this one contained with minimal damage to just one part of the house." He shook his head. "The doors were all jammed from the outside."

Gary's heart ached. "The owner, Monique Harris, this is her dog. Have you seen her?"

"No, but we think she got out through the bedroom. A rocking chair was thrown through the window and a pillow put over the sill. Pretty smart thinking."

So where was Monique?

He glanced down at the dog. "I know you've only been with her a few days, but you're a good dog. Show me where she is. Find Monique." He let go of the collar.

Lord, please let me find her. Keep her safe until I do.

Homer took off at a dead run toward the end of the driveway, barking. He stopped suddenly, turned back to look at Gary, barking, then ran toward the road again.

Trying to lead him to Monique? Gary didn't know, but he had no other options at the moment. He kicked his leg muscles into overdrive and sped after the dog.

Adrenaline pushed him to go faster. His thighs burned as he ran as fast as he could over the loose gravel.

Homer took a stance and barked at Mike's cruiser. Had the dog just been trying to tell him Mike was down? Gary bit back the disappointment.

The EMT shut the back door. "He's fine. Coming to. Looks like a chemical was used to knock him out. We've got him on oxygen and will take him to the hospital for monitoring, but I think he'll be just fine."

"Thanks." Gary watched the truck pull away. He stared at the cruiser. Great. Another vehicle to work as a crime scene.

Homer stood at the passenger side of the car, barking and growling.

"What is it, boy?" Gary moved beside the dog, scrutinizing the area.

And then he saw it—drag marks on the ground beside the car, going toward the back of the cruiser.

His heart skipped a beat as he squatted and studied the marks. It had to be Monique. Not much of a scuffle, so either she was overpowered quickly or… Well, he didn't want to consider the other options his training screamed could have happened. He'd have to work the scene later. Right now, a woman's life was in danger.

The woman he was falling in love with.

Man, her head pounded.

Darkness enveloped her. Monique knew she was awake—coherent, but she couldn't open her eyes. A blindfold covered them. She strained to hear. Off in a distant part of the building where she lay, she could just make out a man's voice.

A greasy stench wafted under her nostrils, causing her stomach to heave. She attempted to hoist herself up from her reclining position, but fell against the restraints holding her hands confined. Using her legs, she eased herself into a sitting position.

Fear surged as realization dawned—she'd been kidnapped!

Reverberations of footsteps bounced off the walls surrounding her. Monique's palms sweated. Her heart raced. *He,* whoever he was, drew closer. Her heartbeat echoed in her head. She leaned back against a hard object—a wall?—and felt cold steel dig into her spine.

She still had her gun! Whoever had her must not have checked. Must have thought she had raced out of the burning house without taking anything.

Shuffle, step. Shuffle, step.

His breathing sounded strained, coming in bursts and pants. She could smell an undertone of fuel in the close room. If only her hands weren't tied in front of her, she could reach her 9 mm. She struggled against the restraints and detected a little play in the knots.

Shuffle, step. Shuffle, step. Step, stop.

Panic overtook her. While she couldn't see through the blindfold, she could *feel* his presence. Feel his stare. She worked her hands faster.

Harsh hands yanked the fabric covering her eyes. She blinked several times, trying to focus in the dim room. Why, she was in Spence's church.

But who was the man standing in front of her?

He was shorter than her five-foot-five-inch frame and looked to be early to mid-thirties. Very slight build, with a thick head of hair. Yet, she didn't recognize him.

His scowl was very intimidating. "You've caused me quite a bit of trouble, Mrs. Harris. Guess it's time to return the favor."

Dear Lord, I know we just got back on an even keel, but please help me.

She stiffened her spine and mustered all her strength, pushing it all into her voice. "You have the advantage—you know who I am, but I don't know you."

He rolled his eyes. "Who I am isn't important."

"But you've kidnapped me. Why? I haven't done anything to you."

"No, you haven't. But it's *who* you are that's important."

"I'm nobody. Just a widow trying to rebuild my life with my new family." Tears filled her eyes. Images of Felicia, Luc, CoCo and Spence's faces flashed before her.

And Gary Anderson.

No, she wouldn't give this man the satisfaction of seeing her cry, seeing her broken. She worked her hands until she felt a little more slack.

"And if you'd have stayed in Monroe and forgotten all about your *new family,* you wouldn't be in this pickle."

And then she knew. She froze. "You're Kevin Haynie."

He cocked his hip out. "Very astute."

"Why does my father want me away from Lagniappe? It's not like he's ever coming back here."

Kevin snorted. "Shows what you know. He'll be out within sixty days."

"He murdered his own brother and nephew. Last time I checked, they don't let murderers like that go free."

"You'd be amazed at what the Trahan money can buy, honey. Even an early release, if you know how to work the system."

"But Justin doesn't have any money. It's all in a trust fund that has reverted to Luc and Felicia upon his incarceration."

"Not quite, toots."

Oh, no. That stupid special trust fund for any legal heirs. Now everything made sense. All of it—Kent being murdered, the threats, the fires...all because of Justin Trahan's greed.

"Why kill my husband? How does that have anything to do with the trust money?"

"Ah, I see you've figured a few things out all on your own. Good girl."

"What was the point?"

"We'd hoped it'd distract you. Since Justin rejected you, we'd hoped you'd stay in Monroe and forget all about Lagniappe." He sneered. "We didn't count on you being so stubborn."

Her mouth went dry as her false bravado vanished. She glanced around the church, looking for something, anything, to distract him. Just long enough to work a hand free to get her gun.

"Well, I've enjoyed our little chat, but now it's time for me to get back to work." He lifted the gas can and tossed the contents all over the red carpet covering the center aisle.

Stall him! "Why here? Why not my house?" She ignored the rope burning into her wrists. Just a little more play and she could squeeze her right hand free.

"Couldn't take a chance on you escaping again. Which you did." He trailed the liquid down the aisle and into the entryway. "Besides, Justin's still upset with his niece and nephew. Burning down the church seems a bit poetic, wouldn't you say?"

"Why not just shoot me, the way you shot Kent?" Working her hands against her wrists, she felt a little more slack in the knot.

He sashayed back to her, frowning. "I didn't kill your husband. Justin hired those bozos before I came into the picture."

"So why not shoot me?"

The smile that spread across his face sent icy spiders up her back. "Because I'm not a killer. I give life. I let fire loose, let it breathe and eat and play."

Oh, sweet mercy, this man was insane. She struggled frantically against the ropes.

He pulled out a matchbox, withdrew a match and struck it. The flame danced upward. The scent of sulfur filled the air, mixing with the greasy fuel stench.

Her heart pounded.

"Isn't it beautiful? See how it moves, how it's alive."

She held her breath as the flame ate the matchstick.

Just before it reached his fingertips, he blew out the fire. He smiled. "I love this part…where I'm about to unleash it, but am still holding it back, controlling the beast."

Sick. The man was sick. And she'd better think of something fast before he killed her.

He withdrew another match and held it against the strike-plate.

Her gaze darted around the front of the church. The altar. "Wait."

He let out a sigh, but held the match. "What?"

"At least let me pray before you do this." Finally, only a little left and she'd have her hand free.

Kevin tilted his head, considering. "Why not?" He nodded toward the altar. "Go ahead and pray."

She stood on wobbly feet.

He held the match against the strike-plate. "But no funny stuff, or you go poof."

She dropped to her knees, using the movement to block his view of her hands. Despite the pain, Monique jerked her right wrist free.

Her hands were untied!

But he held the match…he could strike it and drop it before she could stop him. As much fuel as he dumped everywhere, the place would go up immediately—no chance for her escape.

God, help me here. I don't have any other choice but to pull my gun. Please don't let him strike that match.

In a single, fluid movement, she rose and put her weight on her toes, slipped her hand around her gun, spun and held the shooter's stance with Kevin Haynie in her sights. "Drop the matches, now!"

His heart raced faster than the cruiser over the roads to Vermilion Parish Community Church.

Gary couldn't believe it when the dispatcher came over the radio and redirected all available emergency personnel to the church because a Monique Harris had stopped arsonist Kevin Haynie from setting the church on fire and held him at gunpoint.

Well, glory be praised that she had her gun. The woman never ceased to amaze him. And when he saw her, he intended to tell her just that.

After he hugged her to make sure she was really okay.

He whipped into the church's parking lot just seconds before an EMT unit. Not knowing the situation, Gary withdrew his weapon and ran into the church. The smell of gas, grease and sulfur nearly gagged him. He crashed through the entryway into the sanctuary.

And skidded to a stop at the sight before him.

Kevin Haynie sat quietly in the first pew. Monique leaned against the podium, gun trained on Haynie.

If he'd had any doubts that he needed to pursue a relationship with the woman, they were dispelled now.

He rushed forward, handcuffed Haynie and read him the Miranda rights before turning to Monique.

Her copper curls sprang out all over her head. She lowered her gun to the podium and grinned. "About time you showed up."

He drew her into his arms and, ignoring the EMT and fire department personnel filtering through the church, dipped his head and kissed her. Long. Thoroughly. With as much emotion as he could put into a kiss.

She blinked when he backed away. "Wow. Remind me to get taken hostage more often if you'll run to my rescue and kiss me like that."

"Bite your tongue." But he lowered his head and kissed her again.

EPILOGUE

"**Y**ou know, I bet you'll be promoted next week after the sheriff gets back." Monique sat on the swing beside Gary, looking out over the bayou from her backyard. "You did a great job."

"Look at you—you're the one who caught Haynie."

"Only because of information you uncovered." She glanced at their interwoven hands. "You realize your gift saved my life."

"Huh?"

"The rocker. I threw it out the window to get out when the house was on fire and Haynie had me trapped inside."

"Good thing the house was old or it would've never made it through double-paned windows."

"I'm just sick that the rocker burned up."

"I'll buy you a new one."

She laughed and glanced to the house. "They'll finish all the cleanup tomorrow, and will be able to start rebuilding next week. It's a blessing only the front part of the house was damaged."

"I talked to Spence this morning. He said the church's all done, thanks to your funding the job."

She shrugged. "I figured Justin owed them that. I'm quite certain he was livid when he heard I'd pulled all the cash out of the special fund and given it to the church."

He chuckled. "Oh, I'm sure he was."

She snuggled closer, relishing the warmth of his embrace.

"And thank you for getting his request for early release denied so quickly."

"Hey, it was easy to do with all the evidence. Ogburn and Haynie's statements alone sank Justin's ship."

"I'm glad." She stood, tugging him with her. "You know, if I'm going to build a home here, Lagniappe's pretty much stuck with me forever."

He turned her toward him, staring into her face. The warmth in his eyes made her knees go weak. He pulled her into his arms and kissed her.

Now her knees *really* went weak.

Gary pulled back and smiled. "I love you, you know that?"

Happiness surged through her like a wildfire over timber. Tears stung her eyes. "Oh, Gary. I love you, too." And she did. A part of her heart would always belong to Kent, but Gary was in the present. And the future.

He kissed her again, then hugged her. "Yeah, but you just remember who said it first."

* * * * *

Dear Reader,

Thank you for trudging along through the Louisiana bayou once again. I've enjoyed introducing you to the newest member of the Trahan clan, Monique, and sharing her story with you. She's a welcome addition to Lagniappe, wouldn't you say?

Some of Monique's struggles in her anger at God were struggles I've encountered over the past few years. Thank you for allowing me to share part of my spiritual journey with you. I hope you laughed a little, cried a little, and your faith was strengthened by Monique's story.

I love hearing from readers. Visit me at www.robincaroll.com and drop me a line, or write to me at P.O. Box 242091, Little Rock, AR 72223. I invite you to join my newsletter group and sign my guest book. I look forward to hearing from you.

Blessings,

Robin Caroll

QUESTIONS FOR DISCUSSION

1. Monique lost her husband and had to deal with the additional burden that he had died so violently. How do you handle grief?

2. Gary wanted a promotion and set out to prove himself worthy. Have you ever wanted a promotion or a particular job? How did you conduct yourself?

3. Justin denied that he was Monique's biological father. Have you ever been rejected by someone you're related to? Close to? How did you handle the emotions rejection brought up?

4. Felicia and Luc accepted Monique into their family with open arms—no questions asked. If faced with a similar situation, how would you react?

5. Gary appreciated all the sacrifices his mother had made for him as a child. Has anyone made sacrifices for you? How did you show your appreciation?

6. Monique was angry with God because she'd lost both her mother and her husband. Have you ever been angry with God? How did you deal with your emotions?

7. Justin Trahan would stop at nothing to satisfy his greed. Do you know or have you ever known someone who was insatiably greedy? How do/did you interact with this person?

8. Della was a nurturer by nature, but Gary worried Monique might find her overbearing. Do you know someone with a personality similar to Della's? How would you describe her or his attitude?

9. Gary appreciated his fellow deputy's skills and talents, even though he might be in competition with Mike. Have you ever felt competitive toward a coworker? Were you able to appreciate your coworker's skills and/or talents? Why or why not?

10. Monique had to learn to let go of the past to move on to love again. Whether a love is lost by death or other means, losing love can be difficult. Have you ever lost love? What did you do to overcome your loss and move on to the future?

11. Small towns often have a gossip mill, fed by people like the character of Anna Grace. How do you deal with gossip?

12. Gary fumbled around Monique—saying the wrong thing, blurting out things he shouldn't have, and so on. Have you ever acted like that around someone? Share.

13. Parker Fenton gave Monique an odd feeling for no apparent reason. Have you ever felt that way about someone? How did you handle the situation?

14. Even during trying times, and trials we don't understand, God is our protector. How can you back up that statement with Scripture?

15. The rocking chair Gary gave Monique, which later helped her save her life, was special to her. Does something someone gave you have a special meaning to you? Explain.

HISTORICAL

INSPIRATIONAL HISTORICAL ROMANCE

Adelaide Clark has worked hard to raise her young son on her own, and Boston minister Joshua Blue isn't going to break up her home. As she grows to trust Joshua, Adie sees he's only come to make amends for his past. Yet Joshua's love sparks a hope for the future that Adie thought was long dead—a future with a husband by her side.

Look for

The Maverick Preacher

by

VICTORIA BYLIN

Available February 2009 wherever books are sold.

Steeple Hill®

www.SteepleHill.com

LIH82805

Love Inspired
SUSPENSE
RIVETING INSPIRATIONAL ROMANCE

WITHOUT A TRACE   WITHOUT A TRACE   WITHOUT A TRACE

The prime suspect in Ava's brother's murder: Max Pershing, the man Ava Renault has always secretly loved. To help Max, she'll have to overcome their feuding families and expose the truth.

FRAMED!
ROBIN CAROLL

Available February 2009 wherever books are sold.

Steeple
Hill®

www.SteepleHill.com

LIS44326

With an orphaned niece and nephew depending on him, commitment-shy Clay Adams calls upon nanny Cate Shepard to save them all. With God's help, Cate's kind, nurturing ways may be able to ease the children into their new lives. And her love could give lone-wolf Clay the forever family he deserves.

Look for

Apprentice Father

by

Irene Hannon

*Available February 2009
wherever books are sold.*

www.SteepleHill.com

Steeple
Hill®

LI87515

Love Inspired®
SUSPENSE

TITLES AVAILABLE NEXT MONTH

Don't miss these four stories on sale February 10, 2009

ON A KILLER'S TRAIL by Susan Page Davis
When a sweet, elderly lady is found dead
on Christmas Day, rookie reporter Kate Richards
jumps on the story. Detective Neil Alexander can't
figure out the murderer's motive, but he *does* know
that Kate needs watching. They're on a killer's trail.
And who knows what they'll find....

FRAMED! by Robin Caroll
Without a Trace

The prime suspect in her brother's murder: Max Pershing,
the man Ava Renault has always secretly loved. To help
Max, she'll have to overcome their feuding families and
expose the truth.

EVIDENCE OF MURDER by Jill Elizabeth Nelson
The photographs Samantha Reid uncovers in her new store
could be deadly. They present new insight into a cold case
someone wants to keep closed. And when Samantha is
pushed into the spotlight, Ryan Davidson—sole survivor
of the slain family—must intervene to keep her safe.

DEADLY REUNION by Florence Case
Her sister's engaged to a murderer. Police officer
Angie Delitano is convinced of it. Then Angie uncovers
startling new evidence, forcing her to turn to Boone, the
handsome, hardened lawyer she once loved. Now she
has to learn to trust him again—with the case and
with her heart.

LISCNMBPA0109